Erotic Flava

This book is a work of fiction. Names, characters, places, and other incidents are used fictitiously and are from the author's imagination. Any similarities to locales or persons, living or dead and any actual events, is entirely coincidental.

Cover Design: Jahi Graphic Designs

Acknowledgments

I would like to thank God for answering my prayers and giving such a wonderful talent. Without him, none of this is possible.

I would like to thank all the people that believed in me and never had any doubt about my success.

I send hugs & kisses to my husband for all his encouragement and motivation to keep following my dreams. Thanks for those late night talks and massages that soothed my nerves. You're the best husband on earth!

Jahi Graphic Designs, thanks for taking the time to get my book cover together. I got so many compliments on the Erotic Flava book cover, you did your thing! I wish you all the success in the world.

Dedication

This book is dedicated to my café mom friends for all their support and inspiration. I hope you'll enjoy reading it as well as I enjoyed writing it.

To my friends on myspace, I loved your comments and emails. Thanks for keeping it real!

To the ones that purchased the book, Thank you for your support and I hope you enjoyed your free gift that came with it! I know how to treat my readers.

Smooches

Dear Readers,

Thank you for all the support you have given me, and I hope you will continue to be fans. I thank god for giving me a wonderful talent, for being able to express myself through writing.

Keep It Real

Bleu Kashmere

<u>Internet Love</u>

Here I am searching the internet bored as hell with no place and no man to share my time with. I came across this chat room called Love 30's #1; I see all kinds of crazy names and none of them seems to interest me. I decided to log off and call it a night, before I could do that this name pops into room and instantly catches my attention. I clicked on Swaay 33 profile to see what he was all about.

Within seconds his whole profile came through. I enjoyed what I read about him and the picture that was posted on his profile was delicious! He had a body that was out of this world. No love handles, no beer belly, and definitely no flabby arms, his eyes are light brown with a skin tone to match. This brother had it going on! His appearance wasn't the only thing that was appealing, it was his background. He graduated college, he was a war veteran and he worked from home as a graphic designer. I made the first move and sent him an email saying, "Hi my name is Gabrielle and I would like to get to know you better. I viewed your profile and I liked what I saw. I would like to hear from you." I closed his profile and started playing a game on Yahoo. Not to long after I closed his profile, I get an instant message from him.

Swaay33: Hi, how are you?

Gabby717: Hey there, I'm good and you?

Swaay33: I'm ok. What don't you have a picture on your profile? Are you shy or you just didn't want to?

Gabby717: I didn't want to, I don't usually go into the chat rooms, but I was kind of bored tonight. Besides, when I do get on the computer, it's all about business not pleasure.

Swaay33: What made you send me an email?

Gabby717: Your name looked interesting and I was curious.

Swaay33: Oh ok, I see. So I'm just a try out?

Gabby717: Basically yes! Lol

Swaay33: Lmao! That's cute. When can I see a picture of you?

I glanced at my clock and its 1am.

Gabby717: It's late and I have to get up early, I guess we will talk at a later time. I'll send you an email with my picture and phone number, is that cool.

Swaay33: Yeah, that's great! Have a good night and I'll talk to you later.

Gabby717: Good night.

I logged off the instant messenger and sent him a quick email with my picture and number. I turned of the computer and went to bed with a smile.

My alarm goes off; I go into my children's room and wake them up. I have four beautiful children, two boys and two girls. My mornings are hectic but I love being a mom, I wouldn't have it any other way. As I get the kids together, I'm constantly thinking about Swaay. After my last relationship, I didn't think I would want to even look at another guy. I do have needs and I'm tired of playing with myself at night. All I want is a nice guy that I could enjoy life with and be happy.

The kids are finally dressed and ready for school. Of course my 1 year old stays home with me for now, he'll be in daycare very soon. I took the kids to school and when I get back there's a message on my answering machine. I press play and I hear this soft but deep voice on the other end, "Hey it's Swaay, call me when you get a chance." That made my morning; I waited 10 minutes before I called him back. I was nervous at first but I shook it off, my mother always said, "Always finish what you started, never leave anything half ass, including men." I dialed his number, the phone ringed twice and he answers "Hello." "Good morning, how are you? This is Gabby717." "I know who you are, I'm fine. If you don't mind I would like to know your real name." "Oh ok, my name is Gabrielle and what's yours?" "My name is Taron Styles. So Gabrielle, tell me about yourself." "Well, I have four children, two boys and two girls. I'm divorced; I stay at home with my 1 year for now, until I decide what to do next. I love reading, writing and cooking. Sometimes I like to go out and have a good time. What about you Taron?" "I'm also divorced, I have a daughter with my ex wife. I was in the army, I'm a college graduate and I work from home. Before I go any further there is something that I have to tell you, I was locked up for a little while. I couldn't get a job because of that, so I went to school and got my shit together and went to school. I understand if you change your mind about getting to know me, I just wanted to be honest with you." "I appreciate your honesty; I don't judge people, we all make mistakes and life goes on. Well since we're sharing life experiences, I have one that I left out. My youngest son is by another man, he's been out of my life since my son was born and I don't plan to look for him. My son is fine without him!" "Why did you break up with him?" "I was tired of the lying, cheating and constant fighting. What really put the icing on the cake was when he stayed out for a whole week, he didn't call, he wouldn't answer my phone calls and that's when I knew it was time for him to go. I could do bad by myself, I didn't need him around to make things worst. All he did was stress me out; I wish I never met him!

"Wow, that's deep! Well at least you can start over and forget about him. In life we as people make crazy decisions, we find out later that the situation we were in could've been avoided or we learn from it. I guess you live and you learn." "Yeah that sounds about right, because I surely learned my damn lesson." "I hear yah! After my divorce, I started dating again. In the beginning everything was ok but after a year that's when shit got bad. I was messing with this chic that I went to school with, she was nice and also bi-sexual. There were times when I would come home and find her with a naked girl in our bed waiting for me, so of course I took the bait. She would watch us fuck and then she would join in. That was something we were into at the time and I was young. A year into the relationship she started smoking crack and sniffing cocaine, I wasn't comfortable with her new lifestyle, so I broke it off. She was getting out of hand. I guess we're perfect for each other; we both had some crazy shit going on in our lives." "I guess your right Taron, I just want to be with someone that is sincere and of course they'll have to accept my children." "I really enjoy talking to you Gabrielle; I get a good vibe from you. I would like for us to meet if it's possible." "I would love to meet you. My kids are going to spend the weekend with their father, I'll only have the little one with me, is that ok with you?" "Sure I would love to meet him as well; I guess it's a date."

"Where should we meet?" he asked. "I'm not that far from Jamaica Avenue, I guess in front of Old Navy at 1:00pm on Saturday." "That's perfect." "Well, I have to errands to run and I know you have things to do, give me a call around 10:00pm tonight." "Will do, have a good day and I'll talk to you later." "You too, bye."

I had a busy day; I went food shopping and

paid my bills. All there's left for me to do is feed the kids and put them to bed. I need a vacation bad!

"Ok kiddies it's about that time! I made sure everyone brushed there teeth and tucked them into bed. I always leave a night light on in their room, I said good night to them and closed their door half way. I put on my pajamas and lie on my bed.

The phone rings exactly at 10:00pm; I desperately grabbed the phone and answered it in a sexy voice. "Hello." "Hey Gabrielle, were you sleeping?" "No I was just laying here waiting for you to call." "Oh really?" "Yes really!" "Girl, you got me cheesin over here!" "That's good!" "Gabby, I forgot to ask you something, where do you live?" "I live 89-22 161 street apt 1f, that's right off 89th Avenue." "Wow, I know exactly where that's at! I didn't know you lived so close to me, I live 110-77 176th Street and 110th Avenue. Oh ok, I know the area very well, you can get on any bus that comes down Merrick Blvd to Jamaica Ave." "Yep!" "That's cool, so Taron what do you like to do for fun?" "I like to eat dinner where they play jazz music, I like to roller blade in Central Park on the weekends. But most of all I like to stay home with my lady and make love to her all day & night."

"Are you throwing me a hint?" "Yes, did you catch it?" "I sure did!" "What about you Gabrielle?" "Well, I like to go to different street festivals, I love cooking, reading, shopping. What I like to do most is stay home and watch a good movie. I take my children to Holiday Parades in Manhattan, there's a lot that I like to do." "That sounds interesting; I hope I can do some of those things with you and the kids." "Maybe one day you will. It's time for me to go, you know the drill." "Yeah, I know, I'll call you tomorrow." "Ok have a good night." "You do the same, Goodnight." I hung up the phone and went to bed.

I got up the next morning and did my usual routine. I just got back from taking the kids to school and I have a lot to do. I sat my son on the couch and took off his coat and hat. I turned on the television to his favorite show; he's a good kid it doesn't take much for him to sit quietly. I went in the kitchen and started cleaning, I here a knock on the door. I was surprised because I wasn't expecting anyone, I answered it in a low tone, "Who is it?" "It's Taron." What the fuck! I didn't tell him to come to my house. I opened the door and this fine ass bald head guy was standing there with a sexy grin on his face. I had to catch myself from drooling. "Wow what a surprise! I didn't know you were coming over, please come in and have a seat." He walked into the living room and sat next to my son. "Hey little man, what's up?" My son turned to him and waved hello. "I wanted to see you, I'm sorry I didn't call." "It's ok I'm happy to see you, well while you're here you can help me clean up." We both burst into laughter, but he did help me clean. I thought that was really cool because I didn't expect him to help, I was just messing with him.

"I guess little man was tired, he's knocked out!" he said. I looked over by the couch and my son was in a deep sleep. I picked him up and laid him down in his room, I closed the door half way. I went back into the living room and he was watching television. "Are you hungry Taron?" "Yeah, I'm starving!" he replied. "Come sit at the table while I make us something to eat." he walked over to the table and sat down. I heated the chicken along with rice & beans in the microwave. Taron came into the kitchen and got the forks, napkins and soda and put them on the table. I brought out the food. We talked while we ate, I got to know more about him and I told him more about me. We had a good time and I felt secure with him.

After a few good laughs and jokes, he looked at me and said, "You got something on your mouth." *Before I could take it off, he leaned over and licked the food off my lips. Oh God, why did he do that?! My pussy got so wet that I could smell my sweet juices. I stuck my tongue out to taste his lips; he sucked my tongue as if it was candy. We began to kiss passionately; I pushed my plate away from me and broke the kiss. "What's wrong baby?" "Oh nothing everything is fine, I just got overwhelmed with passion. I don't think we should do this, we barely know each other. But on the other hand, I do want you!" "This is crazy for me too baby; I want you so bad that I could taste you. We're both adults and you have absolutely nothing to worry about. We both want each other, so why fight it? I want to make love to you." I started pacing the floor back and forth; he walked over to me and stroked his hands down my face. "I want you and I know you want me!" he whispered in a sexy tone. I moved close to him and began to kiss his soft lips.*

We stood there kissing each other for awhile, he cupped my breast firmly. I pulled off his shirt and began to unbuckle his pants. I stuck my hand in his boxers and grabbed his dick; I stroked it firmly as he fingered me. Damn he got a dick on him I thought to myself. He yanked my pants down and bent me over the couch; licked my pussy from behind. He made her all wet and slippery. He stopped and beg—an to put his dick into me, it wasn't an easy task. I was so tight and the force of his dick began to hurt, but I refuse to let him stop. He pushed and pushed until he broke through, damn I felt like a virgin. I moaned as if I was in heat. I never had a man that had so much dick. Our bodies were holding a conversation and nothing else mattered at that time.

I yelled "Fuck me harder! Don't stop! Give it to me!" He did exactly what I told him to do. He slapped my ass and pumped me harder and harder, my body was telling his body to fuck the shit out of me. "Scream my name baby!" he requested. I screamed his name loudly, oh Taron I'm cumin!" "Oh shit baby girl, I'm getting ready to bust!" It was like music to my ears, we both came together, the music we made sounded so sweet. I finally found a man that I could enjoy sex with.

My legs became weak and I fell on the couch, he came tumbling right on me. We both laughed and he kissed my back. He got up and walked to the bathroom, I was right behind him. I gave him a wash cloth and we took a hot shower together, we washed each other. The way we were acting, you would've thought we knew each other for years; I guess this is a sign of us being more than fuck buddies. I wrapped the towel around me and told him to go to the bedroom. I went in the living room to get our clothes. I entered the room and there he was staring at me. "What's wrong? "Nothing, I'm just admiring your figure, I love thick women." "I'm glad you do and I like a man that could handle me." We both smiled. "Baby girl, I would like to ask you a question if you don't mind." "Sure, what's on your mind?" "I really like you and I'm comfortable with you as well, I want to know if you would like to build a romantic relationship?" "So, you want us to be together?" "Yes, I'm ready to have a girlfriend again." "I guess we could give it a try, I would like to be your woman." "I promise, you won't regret it. I believe we were meant to meet each other." Deep in my heart I wanted to be with him as well, but I never thought after one day of spending time together, we would become a couple instantly.

Finally my son woke up and I got him dressed. All three of us went to go get the other kids from school. He put my son on his neck until we reached the school. I've never felt so comfortable around someone that I just met; the strange thing is that it feels right and I'm willing to take a chance. Maybe he is the one for me, but only time will tell.

The kids saw mw at the door and came running out like they always do. I introduced then to Taron, they said hello and began talking about going with their dad for the weekend. We reached home and I told them to wash their hands before they got a snack. All their things were packed; all I was waiting for was a phone call from their dad.

Two hours passed and the phone rings, I picked it up and it was their dad. "I'm downstairs, are they ready?" "Yeah, I'll be down in a second." "Ok kiddies, your dad is here let's go!" I yelled. Taron played with little man while I helped the kids with their bags.

Look at this shit! I see this asshole has a new SUV, every time I ask him for extra money for the kids, he always says he can't afford it. I didn't sweat it; I just put the kids in and went back in the building. My weekend was starting off right and I wasn't going to let some small shit like that spoil it. I opened the door and I see Taron sitting there with my son; it felt good to have a man around the house. I sat next to them and we watched television and had a good time.

I guess we don't have to meet on Jamaica Avenue, because he's here with me. I had all types of feelings about us getting together too soon, but it feels right this time. He met my kids and he hit it off with the baby, he's the only face that they'll ever see in my house. I don't believe in bringing different men around kids, that can damaged them.

For the first time in my life, I'm happy with my decision and we're going to be just fine!

Thugbian

*It finally happened; I had sex with a woman!
The way she handled me was better than any
man I fucked with in my life. I'm still in shock
that I let a woman fuck me! This is so out of
my character, but I enjoyed it a lot.*

*Everything happened so fast. I can't tell
anyone about this little fling I had with a
woman. People would start to think that I'm a
lesbian. Even though it happened once,
people would label me as a Lesbos and I can't
have that.*

*Did I cheat on Antoine with a female? Nah! I
don't consider that cheating. I consider it that
to be a wrong decision I made. Even if it was
considered as cheating, it's his fault anyway!
He's always accusing me of doing things that
I normally wouldn't do. All of this could've
been avoided if he didn't make me upset! He is
the reason why I ended up in Sunni's bed.*

*It all began when Antoine and I were at home
drinking and having a nice time. We started
watching the L word, that was my first time
watching the show and it looked very
interesting. All of a sudden he started yelling
and screaming like he was losing his mind!*

"Why are we watching this lesbian shit? I don't want to see bitches licking each other pussy! I beg you to watch porn with me and you give all kinds of excuses on why you don't like porn! Oh I know why you're so into this shit; you got a thing for Sunni! I fucking knew it, you nasty bitch! That shit pissed me the fuck off! How is he gonna accuse me of having a "thing" for Sunni? I know he lost his mind now! I'm so tired of his dumb as remarks, I'm about to let his ass have it! "What the fuck is your problem? You are always saying some dumb shit! Do I say anything about you and Marco spending time together like two fucking faggots? I don't care if ya'll hang out, that's your friend and I expect that. I grew up with Sunni, so of course where close! I don't have time to deal with your bullshit!" "Are you calling me a faggot? I ain't no fucking faggot! Fuck you bitch! You could suck my dick!" "What fucking dick? You have to grow one for me to suck! I can't take this shit anymore, I'm out of here!"

I grabbed my keys and went down stairs to Sunni's apartment. I knocked on the door twice. She finally opens the door. "Hey what's poppin bitch? I'm surprised that your man of yours let you come down here." "Well, we just had it out big time. He's trippin because I watching the L word. He started yelling and calling me bitches and shit! I couldn't take much more of that shit, so I left. I think this is it for us, we both need to move on. I never beef at him when Marco comes over and they go hang out. I would never understand him." "What you need to do is get rid of him! He's a fucking jerk! Yo check this out, I taped me and Carmen fucking last night. Yo that bitch is bad! She knows how to eat some pussy, but she ain't better than me! I had her climbing the fucking walls in here!" "I don't want to see that shit! I don't see the point of being a lesbian anyway, I think it's crazy." "Keep your comments to yourself." "Sorry I was just voicing my opinion, I didn't mean to piss you off." "It's cool. So what are you up today?" "Nothing much girl." "I'm watching the L word on the demand channel, care to join me? "Hell yeah!"

We went in her bedroom and she put the show on. I climbed in bed with her, we both were into the show. There was one episode where this chick was sucking on another woman tit and finger popping her, I started to get warm inside and my pussy released it juices. I was amazed at how two women could fuck each other and be so passionate about it. I guess I have to be a lesbian to understand. Sunni began to touch my breast, *any other time I would've slapped her but I didn't stop her. It felt good and I began to feel horny. She moved forward to give me a kiss and I turned away and said "No kissing! I'll let you do other things to me but I can't kiss you." "Ok I could get with that! Can I eat your pussy? I want to taste you." "Yeah you could do that."*

I removed my clothes and laid on the bed with my legs opened. She began to eat me, her tongue action ain't no fucking joke! Damn this bitch is doing her thing! I know what I'm doing is wrong but I can't help to enjoy this shit. After I came, she began to fuck me with her strap on dick. I imagined her being a guy and let myself go into ecstasy. Sunni is a pretty chick, so I just transformed her into a guy in my mind, but in reality she dress like a man and wears a short hair cut like a man. Her jeans are always hanging off her ass, I call her a thug. She can act gangsta at times. This one of those times where she is showing me her manly side. We went at it for an hour. After everything had happened I started to feel like shit! I got up and put my clothes on.

"Are you ok?" she asked. "No, I'm not! I don't know what the fuck I'm doing! This was wrong and I shouldn't be here, I have to go!" "I didn't force you to do anything, you came

down here feeling like crap and I wanted to perk you up a little bit. If you wasn't comfortable about doing it, why did you go through with it?" "I don't know. I'm sorry that I lead on you. I didn't mean to." "Don't worry about it, we're still cool with each other and this is our little secret." "Thanks Sunni." I'm gonna go up stairs and see if this idiot is still there. I'll see you later." "Aight, be easy chica, call me if he starts his bullshit again." "I sure will, see yah."

I went back to the apartment; I was ready to confront Antoine about out argument. I opened the door and I hear soft music playing, I thought he was surprise me by being romantic. I went in the bedroom and I couldn't believe fucking eyes, Antoine was bent over on the bed while Marco was fucking him like crazy! He was getting his back dug out! I tip toed out the room and called Sunni, she had to see this shit. Within seconds she was in my apartment, I directed her to my room. She looked in the bedroom and her eyes almost popped out of her head. She whispered "I told you he was a fucking fag! I know a fruit when I see one!" Before I could pull her away, she ran up on Marco and started beating his ass. I grabbed a stick and began to beat the hell out of Antoine, he was running around like a little bitch yelling and ducking his head. He ran out the room, Marco finally got away and started cursing us out. "What the fuck! Don't get mad at me because I fuck him better than you! He loves the way my dick feels in his ass, he's tired of your stink ass pussy!" "My pussy don't stink you fucking faggot! Get the fuck out my mother fucking house bitch!" He goes into the living room to see if his sweetie pie was ok. All I could do is laugh, because this is the type of shit you'll see in movies.

We followed behind them, Antoine and Marco were dressed and I notice some bags by the door. I guess he's living me for his new lover. I really don't care, I'm glad I know what he's all about and I could definitely move on. He looked at Sunni and said "I guess you're happy that I'm out the picture you fucking wanna be dude!" "I know what I am, I don't have to hide my sexuality from nobody! Everybody knows I love pussy! As for you, do you know what you are? No you don't, because if you did you wouldn't be in denial about being a fucking faggot! Are you afraid to come out of the closet?" "I'm not a faggot, I'm a man!" "Nigga, please! Real men don't bend over, men like the way a pussy smells, feels and taste." "What the fuck are you?" "I'm a thugbian motherfucker! Keep talking shit and you'll see how manly I can get!

Antoine didn't give no response, he just rolled his eyes, picked up his bags and left. I was so relieved to see him go; there was not one sad bone in my body!

After all the madness had calm down, I turned to Sunni and asked her "What the fuck is a thugbian?" she replied "A thugbian is lesbian that has the thug swagger and could throw down like a man. I'm thugged out like any nigga out there, the only difference is that I'm a chic that loves women." she just taught me something new. I never heard of a thugbian until now.

Once again, I'm single and enjoying my life. I go on a few dates here and there. I haven't had anymore sexual episodes with Sunni, as a matter fact her girlfriend Carmen now lives with her. I'm happy for them. I know one thing, the next time I get involved with another man; I'm going to do a serious background check. Antoine taught me a good lesson.

Quickie

"Oh baby, go deeper! Fuck me harder you bastard! I want to feel you in my gut! Oh shit baby I'm cuming! Oh shit! Oh shit! Oh shit! Ahhh that's what I like! Mmm... I love a good morning fuck! Baby that was great!" "Yes it was! What time is your husband coming home?" I took a quick look at the clock and its 6:45am. "Oh shit you gotta go; he'll be here in an hour! Get up and put your shit on!" "Damn girl!" I almost pushed him on the floor. I'm not taking a chance on getting caught. If he had his own apartment I would've been over there instead of him coming here. Well that's what I get for fucking with a young boy! I guess it serves me right.

He finally gets his shit and leave. I took a hot shower and started getting ready for work. I remembered that I have to change the sheets; this has to be done before he comes home. I want to act as if everything is normal. I have to slow down and catch my breath. I don't want him to see panting like a dog.

I'm not happy with my marriage. I've been through so much shit with him over the pass three years and I'm just tired of the bullshit. I'm seriously thinking about leaving him.

In the beginning everything was fine. We had so much in common. The sex was off the hook! He brought me out of my shell. I haven't had a lot of men in my life to know what good sex was all about. The men I've been with came from Small Ville. They didn't have enough to satisfy my sexual desires. When I hooked up with my husband, I knew he was the one to keep me satisfied. The power of his dick hypnotized my body and calmed my soul. He made me into a woman.

Our relationship fell apart because of his passion for drugs. He started staying out late on pay days. It got so good to him that he spent a weekend out in the streets smoking crack. I gave him so many pictures to get his life together. In the mist of all, he has cheated on me with an ex girlfriend. This bitch had the nerve to send me an email about their relationship and she suppose to have a baby girl that belongs to him. This made me sick to my stomach. I confronted him about it and everything got out of control. He admitted to the affair and denied the child. He promised me that he was going to get help and never did! I guess he doesn't care about our marriage and neither do I. I'm just going to do me.

I'm seeing this other guy that I fuck with at

work. I will be doing some overtime tonight.

I hear the door open. "Hey babe, where are you?" he calls out. "I'm back here getting ready for work." I yelled out. I go out to greet this fucking piece of shit. "Hey boo, how was work? " It was cool, nothing much happened last night." "Oh ok. Well I have to go, I'm running late. I have a meeting after work; I'll be home a little late." "Ok babe, be careful and I'll see you later." "Bye baby." Boy am I such a good liar! He believes anything I tell him. I wouldn't be this way if he didn't fuck around behind my back. He wasn't thinking of my feelings when he fucked his ex girlfriend. He got real sloppy with his dirt! At least I have the common sense to use protection; I'm too good to get caught!

I have my own office and no one knocks on my door when my shade is closed. When I arrive to work early, I lie on my chaise chair and fall asleep for hours and no one knows that in in there until I come out. It feels good to be the boss of my department.

I got myself I fine piece of meat that I can't wait to get my hands on tonight! We usually go to the hotel, but I want to explore some office loving with him. Every time I think about him my pussy gets wet. The sound of his voice sends me to orbit! I shall get what I want tonight and more. He already know what time to come see me and he knows what I like. He could have all he want tonight!

Time flies when you're having fun, it's already 6:00pm and I'm ready to get broken off in the worst way. I see him walking towards my office and I start breathing heavy. He just turns me on! I love the way he walks. He has this sexy swagger and this arrogant way about him. All I want to do is give him a good fuck! No conversation just straight sex.

He opened the door and said "Did you want to see me?" "Yes, come in and lock the door." he did want I told him to do like a good boy. "Take off your clothes and lay on the floor!" I commanded. I love being in control. I straddled him and gave a fuck that he would never forget. He has a long black dick that pokes my pelvic bone. It's painful at times, but I'm a freak and pain is pleasure. He held my waist tight as we went into overdrive. "Yes baby, that's it take it like a man! That's right make me cum baby! Do what the boss says! Oh you young mother fucker! Oh shit! Oh shit! Oh! Oh! Oh! Oh god I'm fucking cuming! I screamed so loud that he had to cover my mouth. Damn this boy knows how to fuck! He keep fucking me like this, I won't need my sorry ass husband anymore. I got up and cleaned myself up and said "You can go now, we're done for today. I will let you know when I need you again. Thanks for a wonderful evening." He smiled and fixed his clothes. He walked to the door and said "Your welcome and I'll see you soon." I gave him a devilish grin as he walked out the door.

I gather my things and headed home to that sorry ass husband of mine. I could sleep well tonight with a smile on my face. Two quickies in one day, now that's fulfilling!

Fuck Buddy

Leon and I have been friends for 10 years, we work at the same jobs and we talk about everything. We also do special favors for each other. When I feel my juicy Lucy twitch, I call him to calm her down. He satisfies all of my needs.

We both are single and were not ready to be in a relationship at the moment. He always tells me how sexy I am and the way I speak Spanish to him while we're fucking drives him crazy.

One night it was raining and I couldn't sleep, I called Leon to see if he would come and put me to sleep. The phone rings about three times and he finally answers. "Hey girl what's up?" "Nothing much, I can't sleep so I decided to give you a call." "I know what you need; I'll be down stairs in a minute." That's my boy! He knows what I need and is always ready to give it to me.

The bell rings and I go and open the door. He has on his lounge pants and no shirt on. His body is nice and tight. That made me wet! He goes straight to the bedroom and I followed behind him. We did our favorite position, which is 69. As he licks my pussy I deep throated his dick. He has a nice size dick but the head of it is extremely huge. I took it all in and it drove me crazy! I was really enjoying myself. The feeling became so intense. I shouted "Aye dios Mio!" I came so hard that my chest started to hurt. I continued to suck his sweet dick and shortly after me he came. He filled my mouth with cum. It was sweet and I swallowed every bit of it.

He flipped me over and started fucking me doggy style. The tip of his dick swells every time we fuck. I love it when he goes deep. We both reached our climax. We were so loud; I thought the neighbors heard us. I don't care if they did. I was getting my fuck on!

We talk about who's fucking who on the job. About an hour later I told him that it was time for him to go home and get ready for work. He agreed. He kisses me softly and said "See you at work." "Ok sweetie." I replied. I smiled as I locked the door and returned to my bedroom. My body was tired but it was worth it. Maybe one day we will be together as a couple, but as for right now I'm enjoying him as my fuck buddy.

Erotic Thoughts

&

Behavior

More stories By Bleu Kashmere

New story by Jahi

<u>Anonymous Letters</u>

Damn I have to get this off my chest; I'm feelin three guys that I want to fuck. I'm trying to figure out a way to tell them without exposing myself. Hmmm...... I got it! I'll just write them a letter. That's the only way I can get their attention and keep them on their toes.

My life is so boring right now and I have to spice it up! I love my boyfriend, but he's not doing anything to bring back the spark in our relationship. I guess if you want something done you have to do it yourself.

I turn on my computer and began to write my letters to the men that will be my victims. Yes, I'm going make these men my sexual slaves.

Dear Phinese,

You might think this is a little strange, but I just want to let you know how I feel about you. I've known you for three years and I never had the heart to confront you face to face. We are both in situations, you have a wife and I have a boyfriend but that doesn't change the way I feel about you. Every time I come to the club and see you guarding the door, my panties become wet! All I think about is taking you in the bathroom and give you a good fuck! Damn, just thinking about sneaking around with you turns me on! I just want the chance to show you that I can be more than a friend. I'm not trying to steal you away from wifey, I just want some of what she's getting!

If you're curiosity is getting the best of you, that means you want to know who I am. All you have to do is meet me at the Double Tree hotel right off the conduit. Expenses will be paid for, be there at exactly 10pm. I'll be in room 300. See you there baby!

                                    Secret lover

Ok that's one down two more to write. I hit the print button and proceed to write the second letter.

Dear Leonidas,

I'm always coming into your restaurant and order my favorite lunch. When I'm sitting there eating my food, I imagine us on the table doing sensual things to each other! I would love to such your dick with whip cream on top. I never had a Greek man before and I want you to be the first. I don't know if you have someone in your life and it doesn't matter to me at all! I want you bad! I have to have you! I want you to feel this chocolate pussy on your dick. Just think for a moment, I'm on top of you going up and down, moving in circular motions, squeezing my pussy on your joy stick! Ok that's enough; I painted a picture for you now do something for me.

I'll be waiting for you at the Double tree hotel Friday night at 11pm. Go to room 300. Can't wait to see you!

Chocolate

I have one more letter to complete my mission. I'm such a scandalous bitch!

Dear Carlos,

Hey boo! What's poppin? I'm not gonna beat around the bush!

Since I was 16 years old, I had a major crush on you! I want you bad papi! I missed you while you were locked up, now that you're home, I have a gift for you. The only way for you to get it is to meet me. I'm a grown ass woman that knows what she wants. I'll be waiting for you on Friday at 12pm at the Double Tree hotel (the one your mom use to work at), come to room 300. I'll be waiting for you.

Mocha

I hit the print button again to print out the two letters. I put them together and place them in the envelopes. I will mail these on my way to work tomorrow. I'm not nervous, but I am excited! I can't wait for this to go down.

My reservations are in place, all I have to do is just go there early Friday afternoon and turn the room into a pleasure palace.

Let's Get This Party Started

I just got off work and I'm getting my bag packed and ready for tonight's hook up. My heart is beating fast and my hands are sweating. I need a drink to calm me down. I walk over to the bar and pour me a drink. Mmmm... it's nothing better than a shot of Hennessey going down with no chaser, that'll do the trick for now. I'm not a drinker, so a shot will put me in a mellow state of mind.

My front open and I hear keys rattling. "Babe I'm home!" oh shit its Matthew (my boyfriend). "What the hell is he doing here so early?" I said to myself. "Hey honey, I'm in the bedroom." I yelled out. He came in the room and gave me a kiss. He had an Olive Garden bag and the food smelled good. "Oh what's this you got here?" I asked jokingly. "I thought I'll stop and get some dinner, so we can stay in and have a romantic dinner tonight." "Aw that sounds sweet but I have to go out tonight and help a friend of mine get ready for her party. Why didn't you tell me you had plans boo?" "Well, I thought I would surprise you. I didn't know you had plans." "I tell you what, why don't you spend the night. I'll take a shower while you set up the table for dinner. We could eat early and have drinks. When I get back form helping my friend, I'll give you a dessert you'll never forget." I said while nibbling on his ear. "That sounds like a plan baby!" he replied as he rubbed my ass. The touch of his hands let me know that he wanted a sample before I got in the shower.

I unbuckled his belt and put my hand in his pants. I started to jerk and massage his dick.

That turned him on more and more. He removed my hand and pushed me on the bed. He pulled down my pants along with my panties and commenced to fucking me. He gave it to me good, but there's a down fall to his fucking. After five hard pumps, he explodes! This is very aggravating! Before I can get into it, he cums and it's a done deal for him. This gave more gusto to go do my thing tonight. One of these men has to give me what I'm looking for sexually. I can't deal with this five pump shit any longer. I'm gonna let all of my freakiness out on these men, I hope they can handle it!

I go in the bathroom and leave my sorry ass lover on the bed snoring. I'm glad he had fun because it did nothing for me. I pin up my hair, turn on the shower, brush my teeth and turn down the light. Yes we have a light switch that turns up and down. I always use the low light for my showers, it makes me feel relaxed. I step in my warm shower and lather my body with peppermint soap. After I lather up a couple times and rinse off, I scrub down with Rosalyn Scent green tea exfoliating scrub. It works wonders, I absolutely love it. It leaves me feeling soft and rejuvenated. I rinsed and now I'm ready to get sexy.

I come out the bathroom in my towel and he

is still sleeping. All I could do is shake my head. He acts as if he put in work. Anyway, I oil down and sprayed some of man catcher perfume on (of course Rosalyn Scent products) and threw on my black wrap around dress. I took down my hair, and comb it all going back and put my gold Panamanian hair clip in. I look at my watch and its 8:00pm. Damn time waits for no one. I grab my bag and head out the door, leaving ole boy in dream land.

I jump in my car and headed over to the hotel. I'll be there in no time. I don't live to far from there anyway. I turn on the radio and jammed to 98.7 kiss fm.

It took me no more than twenty minutes to reach my destination. I have a special parking space that I'm secure with and it keeps my car from being noticed. I put on my lipstick and turn off my cell phone. I don't want to be disturbed by anyone. I get out the car, fix my dress and reach in and get my freak bag. I closed the door and press my lock button on my key chain and head into the hotel.

I walk up to the guest desk and handle my business. "Hey girl, did any confirmations come in yet?" I asked. "Yes and all three have confirmed. Girl, you are a hot mess you!" She replied jokingly. "You didn't know? I was born a hot mess!" we both laughed and I walked to the rooms. I go into room 300 to set up my sensual theme. I covered both beds in pink and red roses. I the handcuffs on the night stand, I filled the room with red strawberry scent candles. I place the baby wipes in the bathroom, just in case they need to clean up. I lit all the candles and turned off the lights, I did a great job hooking up this room. I made sure everything was and in place and I left the room.

My room is next door and Chanel (girl from the guest desk) will call me when my first victim is here, which is soon. She would lead him to the room and let him. I change into my red sheer lingerie and put on my red stilettos. I guzzle my shot bottle of Bacardi lime and lay on the bed. I'm starting to feel relaxed and freaky. I'm definitely gonna get my freak on tonight.

Ten minutes later I get a phone call and it's Chanel. "I'm bringing him now." "Ok thank you. When the rest of them come, just send them to the room and tell them to knock three times. I don't want to over work you." "Oh ok, thanks for being considerate." we both chuckled for a moment and hung up the *phone. I immediately got up and raced out the door. I dodged in the other room so quickly that I was surprised at myself, for moving so fast.*

Mmmm... the room smells nice and I'm ready to fuck! The aroma had overwhelmed me and became horny instantly. I sit on the bed and wait for my victim to come in. The opens slowly and Phinesse walks in. "Hello, I'm here!" he said in a low tone. "I'm here too. Come in! I said in a commanding voice. He walks in looking shy. Remove your clothes and lay on the bed!" I was in control and I wanted him to do whatever I commanded for him to do! He did exactly what I told him to do. I climbed on the bed and straddled him. "I'm so glad it's you. You had my brain scrambling all week!" "Shhh... We have time to talk; all I want to do is fuck!" It felt so good to be in control!

I started to jerk his hard thick dick slowly. My pussy juice is starting to run down, I climbed on top and fucked the shit out of him! He held on to my waist tightly. I can feel him thrust his dick more and more. He was in my guts and I enjoyed it. He began to get rough and flipped me over like a fucking pancake! Now he's on top and fucking me like I stole something! "Damn you got some good pussy!" he shouted. "Come on cum for daddy!" "Oh baby fuck me harder! Beat it up baby! Give it to me papi!" Oh my god, fuck me you chocolate mother fucker! He gave my pussy the ultimate beat down! Ole boy needs to take lessons from him like yesterday.

Within ten minutes I came so hard that tears rolled down my cheek. "Yeah baby that's what I'm talking about! Damn I didn't know you could fuck like that boy!" "I get the job done!" he said calmly. I look at the time and go in the bathroom to freshen up.

I came out and he was still on the bed undress. I didn't mind at all. His body was eye candy for me and I enjoyed looking at it. Everything about him is sexy, from his eyes to his feet. This brother definitely has it going on to the tenth power!

The phone rings and I immediately pick it up. "Hello" I answered. "Hey it's me, we have a situation. Both men are her now. What do you want me to do?" "Well since they're early, just send them in." "Ok, just checking." I hung up the phone and walked to the door. Both men are standing their in confusion and they both look good! I invite them in.

Leonidas and Carlos walk in and see Phinese

in bed butt as naked. "What's going on?" Carlos asked. I started to explain myself. "This is a private party. I invited three men to this hotel that I wanted to fuck and have a good time with. I already fucked Phinese and now I want you and Leoanidas. This is my fantasy that I want to fulfill and you guys should be happy that you're apart of it. So if you feel uncomfortable this is your chance to leave now. If you want this pussy and you're to fuck, well you know what to do!" Carlos and Leonidas started to take off their clothes. While they're doing that I lie on the second bed and open my legs, exposing my bare pussy to them. Phinese jumps out the other bed and dives his face into my kitty. His tongue game is on point and I'm enjoying the pleasure. Leonidas walks over and puts his dick in my mouth and Carlos starts to suck my breast. I hit the jackpot tonight!

I had my way with all three men and they had their way with me. It was fun fucking all three of them and I must say these weren't any minute men. If I was to get pregnant I wouldn't know who will be the father of the child, but I have nothing to worry about because I'm practicing safe sex and having the time of my life.

Four hours had passed and we're just

finishing our sex party. Everyone is getting dressed and cleaning up the room. I sat down and waited for them to leave.

Carlos and Phinese leave first, they both gave me hug and kiss my cheek. "This was a beautiful night, keep in touch." Phinese whispered in my ear. Carlos waits for his turn. "I'm glad I had the chance to give you something special. If you ever need anything, just send a letter." we both laughed and embraced each other for a moment. He leaves and now it's just Leonidas here with me. I noticed he's looking at me, like he wants to tell me something.

"Is everything ok?" I asked out concern. "Yes, I just want to tell you something." "Oh ok, I'm all ears." I sat on the bed and gave him my undivided attention. "It's clear that I didn't know you had these type of feelings for me and I'm cool with it. Well, I have feelings for you too, but mine are stronger and deeper. What I'm trying to tell you is that I'm in love with you. I've been in love with you for a long time. I didn't want to tell you in front of the other guys, that's' why I waited until they were gone." I couldn't believe my ears! I respect the fact he told me this, but damn we can't get into nothing serious. Wow, this is some wild shit right here! I keep my cool and

began to tell him how I feel. "That took a lot of courage to just come and tell me this now. I really respect your feelings, but I have someone that I'm in a relationship with and I'm ready to let it go right now. I am attracted to you and I think you're a very sexy guy. We can be friends for now. I hope I didn't hurt your feelings." "No, I'm cool with how you feel. I would love to be your friend. I hope we have the opportunity to be together again, just us. If you should ever need someone to talk to or a hang out buddy, you know where to find me." "I'm so glad you understand and of course this isn't the last time you'll see me." "Ok it's settled! I have to go and I'll see you soon." he leaned down and gave me a kiss that sent chills through my body. I wanted to grab him and fuck him again while I had the chance. I'll see him again and this time I'll have him all to myself. I guess writing these letters turned out good after all.

Blue Monkey

Party Time

I'm getting ready to go to my friend Maria's house for a dinner party. Every year there's a different theme and drinks to match the theme. This year the theme is Blue Monkey. I never heard of it until she mentioned it to me. I thought about it and it boggled my mind that she would pick such a thing. I couldn't take the curiosity anymore; I had to know about this blue monkey.

Before I put on my shoes I sat on my bed and called Maria on my cell phone. The phone rang twice; she finally picked up on the third ring. "Hello." "Hey Maria what's up?" "Oh nothing, I'm just putting together some last minute items before the guest arrives. What are you doing?" "I'm getting ready to come to your blue monkey party. Let me ask something, what made you pick this theme and what the hell is a bleu monkey?" "Oh my goodness you are so silly! Well if you must know, one of my co-workers came by to chill with me one night. We talked about work and other boring shit. We ate and as the night passed, we got bored. We went to the liquor store and bought different types of vodkas along with some fruit drinks. It was one of those nights where we were kind of bored. Anywhoo we came back to my place and had own our little party. I made the drinks and she rolled the blunts. We smoked the blunts and it didn't give us a buzz at all. Girl, when we got a hold of that blue monkey, it has us feeling right! Once you go blue you'll always stay true! Ever since that night I haven't messed any other drink, I can't cheat on my blue monkey girl! So that's where the idea came from and now I'm giving my friends an experience they'll remember." "After hearing that, I don't think I want any blue monkey!" "Girl put your big girl panties on and get over here! You have to try it." "I'll try it but if I get out of control, please lock me a room somewhere! I'll be there soon let finish getting myself together. I'll see you soon." "Ok girl see yah!" we both laughed while hanging up the phone. This blue monkey got me going and I ain't had none yet.

I put on my shoes, jewels sweater and I left the house. I was on my way to party with the blue monkey. Lol.

I arrive there a half hour later and it was packed! I didn't expect to see this many people at a dinner party, I guess their curiosity got the best of them as well.

I walked around to check out the decorations, everything was wonderful. She really put her all into the theme. I must say this is one of her best themes, I didn't expect it to be so exquisite. I loved the colors of the décor, turquoise and platinum. Everything was so classy.

I saw everyone going to their seats; I found Maria and sat next to her. She was very happy that I made it there and couldn't wait for me to try her drink. We all ate dinner laughed and talk about this blue monkey. It seems to me that all of her co-workers had some of it before. The ones that were talking about looked as if they were craving it.

After awhile Maria stood up to make an announcement. "I just want to thank everyone for coming out and I hope you all had a good time. The waiters are coming around with the drinks, please take it easy and I hope most of you have a designated driver. I hope you will enjoy it, thank you." Everyone clapped for her and started taking their drinks from the waiters as they came around. Maria presented me with her concoction in a tall 8oz glass with umbrellas and little monkey figures on the glass. It was a nice presentation. The drink was a nice deep turquoise color and it had a sweet smell *to it also. I began to drink the blue monkey. It had a smoothie feel to it and the taste of blueberries came to mind. After three sips I began to feel a buzz, I took in about four more sips and I was gone! Everything had turned black! I was having all kinds of weird dreams.*

The Next day

I woke up in Maria's guest room. I couldn't remember a damn thing that happen at the party. I jumped out of bed and went to Maria's room. I opened the door and she was sitting there combing her hair. "Good morning monkey girl!" she said with laughter. "Why are you calling me that? What happened?" "Oh girl, you had us laughing! You were doing some outrageous dance you called the Monkey! You had us rolling!" "Oh no, I don't remember nothing! That's the last time I'll try anything you make!" "You say that now, by the weekend you're going to be asking me for the recipe." "That's what you think! I'm going home, I'll call you later." "Do you need a ride?" "No, I'm good I need to walk off this tipsy feeling." I went in the room to get my sweater; I noticed my sweater was next to a blue gift bag. I picked up my sweater and looked in the bag, it was a bottled of blue monkey she gave out as party favors. I shook my head and smiled, I put the bottle back in the bag and left.

I finally reached home. I'm awake and hungry. I go in the kitchen and made some toast and sausages. After I gobbled that down, I started to crave a taste for blueberries. The only thing I had that would satisfy the taste is a bottle of Blue Monkey. I fought back and forth with myself about drinking it so early. Finally I decided to open it, I'm home and if I pass out so be it! I thought to myself. I grabbed a glass and poured it over some ice; I let it chill for a minute. My minute was up and took it down in one shot! I repeated this until it was gone. I laid back in my chair, put my feet up and let the blue monkey take control of me.

<u>Hot & Juicy</u>

I met a guy that had this wicked and sexy way about him. I invited him over to my house for a drink. He came over and told me straight up what he wanted. I felt the same way.

After our drinks, I took him to my bedroom and started to strip in front of him. He looked at me with hungry eyes. He took off his clothes and laid on the bed. I climbed on top of his dick and started to work it. I fucked him with so much passion. My body was pouring with sweat. He pumped his thick dick faster and harder inside of him. I wasn't gonna let him win this battle, so I rode him faster and faster! My stomach muscles began to tighten. The intense feeling came over me. I began to cum; my sweet juice ran out of me like Niagara Falls. He held on to my hips tighter and fucked me harder. Mmmm..... It's his turn.

Finally he exploded inside of me. Ooooh I love the way his cum feels. So hot and thick just like his dick! That turns me on! He pulled me down to him and said "I will never forget this night! You will always be on my mind!" I gave him a sensual kiss and smiled.

This was only a fuck and I wasn't about to get caught up, but I can tell he did. I just wanted to fuck him to kill my curiosity. He was what I imagined and more.

An hour later he was ready to leave. I escorted him to the door and gave him a hug. He hugged me back and gave me a kiss that let me know he wanted me again. I pushed him away and said "Good Bye." He turned away and I closed the door.

Every time I go on a vacation alone, I always end up in trouble. I guess I have to bring my husband on my next vacation. How do you think I caught him? He got caught up under the spell of my Hot & Juicy pussy.

<u>Halloween Party</u>

I can't wait to go to the party tonight! I go every year and I always have a good time. My girl friend Tammy got me hooked. At first when I went I thought everybody was losing their damn mind. I couldn't believe the things people were doing. I have to admit, she did warn me before we left that it wasn't a normal party. But I thought, how bad can it be? I shrugged it off and went to the party anyway.

Before we left she laid down the rules. "Ok Simone you're sure you want to go to the party? Because there are rules that you have to follow, or else you'll get kicked out!" "Yeah girl! How bad can it be Tammy? "Ok listen up! You are not allowed to remove your mask. No other clothing will be worn unless it's your costume. Everything is confidential. Oh, and one last thing, you are not to give anyone your real name. What's done at the party stays at the party! You feel me?" "I got you. Why is everything so secretive?" "Because this is strictly for adults and we don't need any under aged teens trying to be apart of an adult affair. These people come from all over just to experience this kind of party. When it first started we had ten people there. *Every year it grew bigger; our party is the shit!" "Ok if you say so, I want to see for myself." "Oh you will see, trust me!" she said in a sneaky voice.*

My costume was hot! My friend designed it for me, I like to be original. I wore a red dress with black buttons going down and stopped at the crack of my ass. The top was form fitted and the bottom flowed out. (Think of a 50's or 60's dress but sexy) I had on 4inch red heels with a custom hand bag to match. No panties, bra nor stockings were worn. My double D's sat nicely in my dress; my mask was made out of a velvet material. My outfit was the shit! Nobody could fuck with what I had on! Tammy's outfit was nice but common. She was in love with my costume. "Damn girl, I'm feeling that outfit! Where did you buy it?" she asked. "I had it made; you should know me by now!" "Oh yeah I forgot, little miss have to be different!" "That's right girl!" "It's hot! I really like it!" "Thanks." I replied with a smile.

The party was located in Jamaica Estates; I didn't live far from there. We took a cab and we were there less than 20 minutes. The house was huge and beautiful. It had all kinds of Halloween decorations hanging from and around the house. We walked up to the door;

a guy was standing there with a black suit and a black mask on. Scary and sexy rolled into one. Tammy gave him the invitation and we walked in. It was packed! The music was banging. You could tell the DJ was black. There was so much food and the bar was stocked with liquor. I noticed large glass bowls and vases filled with condoms and body candy. I still didn't think anything of it. People were dancing and having a good time. I felt good being there. I went to the bar and ordered me a drink called Sexy, its sweet and smooth with pieces of fruit mixed in it. I sat there sipping and just feeling the atmosphere.

I noticed this guy staring at me from across the room. I motioned him to come to me. He came over and sat next to me. I began to get nosey. Jokingly I said "I noticed you were staring at me, do you know me? He chuckled and responded, "You got jokes, no I don't know you but you look sexy in that dress. I would like to get to know you, is that a problem?" "No not at all." "So how long have you been coming to these parties?" "This is my third year. What about you sexy?" I love the way he talked. His voice was so deep and smooth. He made me want to drop my panties; oh I forgot I'm not wearing any. "This is my first time, my girlfriend invited me. So far I love it!" "Would you like to dance?" he asked. "Of course!" I was ready to show him my skills. We stepped on the dance floor and danced to that new joint by Timberland (The way I are) that shit had a fly ass beat and it had me losing my mind! I was doing my thing. I was surprise to see him keeping up with me. I was all over him. He started humping my ass and feeling on my breast. I turned around and grabbed a handful of dick and balls. I massaged them gently. The music became more intense. The DJ was on point with hit after hit.

The lights began to dim and the DJ got on the mic, "What's up party people! Give it all you got! Give it all you got! Take it off! Take it off!" I noticed everyone started taking off their costumes. The guy I was dancing with was completely naked; he didn't have much to take off anyway. I was against it at first but I gave it a try. I didn't want to be the only odd ball dancing with a costume on. My body started moving to the beat and within minutes I was naked. This freaky feeling took over my body. We kept dancing. He got close and began to kiss me. I rubbed his ass and jerked his dick. This time the DJ played the extended version of "Taste Your Love." The music itself was sexy and it made you wanna fuck! I kept grinding and jerking on his dick, before you knew it he put inside of me. Yes we *were fucking on the dance floor, and from what I can see we weren't the only ones. I'm very flexible when it comes to having sex. I threw my leg on his shoulder and received a good fuck. His dick was so thick and big. I didn't want him to stop. He turned me around and bent me over, he gave me every inch of his dick and I took it all in. We went at it for an hour. This was my first sexual party experience and I'm glad I came.*

In every part of that house there was some fucking going on. This was no place for regular people. To have a good time you had to be a freak, I fit right into that category. If you're looking to fall in love or build a relationship, well this is the wrong party. This party is strictly for fucking! If you don't want to fuck, don't come to the party! That's how it is. I got to know a lot of people. I fucked a lot of men, I even let Tammy and her friends have their way with me. Shit everybody got a piece of this ass. The best lover out of everybody was the DJ. I wanted him last and I got exactly what I wanted. He fucked me with no mercy. He ate the hell out of my pussy. It doesn't get any better than that. I had an exotic time of my life!

Every year it gets better. This year I know its going to be off the hook! I'm ready for a night of pleasure. Who said Halloween had to be scary, it's a night of freaky fucking! Christmas is no longer my favorite holiday, I replaced it with Halloween!

The Spizot (The Spot)
By Jahi

Jesus!! 12:45? My God, my head feels like it's gonna explode. I think, no I know hangovers are not for me, but it was definitely worth it. Last night was probably the best night of my life.

I'm Jeff, and yesterday I was your average 24 year old man, minus the fact that I was still a virgin. Yes, I waited all those years, for something I was told not to do until I was married, and ironically it came from my mother. It's ironic because she's the reason I'm no longer a virgin. No don't get it twisted, I didn't have sex with my mother, but my mother is the one who introduced sex to me by taking me to a place, where most religious people would call a den of sin. It all probably sounds confusing to you, so let me lay it out to you.

I spent most of my adult life and money dating, in search of finding the right one. I finally realized that something was wrong. Was it me, or them; I still don't know. So what did I do? I went to my mother's house and confided in her. My mother by the way is divorced, and has been for 15 years from my father. She told me, "You're trying too hard and looking in the wrong places. You have to be; otherwise you would have dated a better crop of women." I told her, "mom, all that's fine and dandy, but I need help, not a sermon." She gave me a hard look and told me, "maybe now is not the time for you to find that special one, but it's no reason for you to not have fun, and all the, "no sex till you're married", was told to you because you're young, and having sex before you got yourself together would end any chances of becoming successful. You have, as a black man, to concentrate on getting an education and building up your credit so that after you graduated college and your credit was excellent, life would be easier for you and you wouldn't have to struggle like I did." She then told me she might have the answer to my dilemma, but she needed a couple days to figure it out. Answer to my dilemma? Figure it out? What the fuck!

Two days later my mom called me at my job and told me to stop by before I went home, because she wanted to talk to me in reference to our previous conversation. Damn, she acted like the phone was bugged. Anyway, I agreed and spent the rest of the day looking at the damn clock wishing the day would end already.

Well, what a conversation it was. I learned that my mother, the one who breast fed me, the woman who wiped my ass when I couldn't, was going to an after hours spot for about six years, and was having consensual sex with strangers; men and women. After the initial shock, I asked her why she was telling me this, and the answer I got shocked the shit out me. She wanted to take me there, introduce me to one of her female friends, and pay for me to fuck her at a place they call, "the Spizot (spot)". Whoa! Go mom! My dumb ass told her to give me a day to think about it, knowing full well that I was down, shit my dick was hard as Chinese arithmetic. I guess it was because it was coming from my mom, the one who breast fed me, the woman who wiped my ass when I couldn't. Even now I keep thinking that. But guess what? The very next day, after no deliberation on my part, I told her yes, I'll go.

We pulled up to this nice ordinary large house. It was so ordinary; I asked my moms if we were picking the chic up first. She laughed and told me, "no silly we're here and so is she. I called before I picked you up to make sure she was in and getting ready." I say it again, go mom!!

We get inside and in the porch stood a counter, and next to it was the finest sister I ever saw. She also might have been the finest because I never saw a half naked woman with my bare eyes before. She had on a two piece lingerie set, and I could see right through both pieces. Her tits hung perfectly, her nipples were hard her areolas were huge, her legs had the look of an Olympic runner, she had the line on the side of her leg to show the muscle separation, and her calves were sick. Her whole body was shining from baby oil. Beam me up Scotty! Instant hard on. She stood there, glistening in the light with one leg crossed over the other. She opened her leg, I guess to advertise, and I could see the shape of her pussy through the lingerie. My mom introduced us to each other, and I had to try to hide my excitement swelling in between my legs. She then told us to get acquainted while she took care of the bill. Candy, I found out was her name, gave me a strong as drink straight, no chaser. She told me it'll make me last longer and help with any weird feelings. I took it and downed it. My stomach burned like there was a fire in it. I thought about what was to come and took another shot. Candy then grabbed my dick. "Ooh baby, your mother didn't tell me you were holding like this. I'm gonna have to make sure I have magnums back there." I felt like I was gonna come in my pants right there. I took her hand away and went to my mother. I asked her what was taking so long and she told me that she was just paying for the room. She had this shit eatin' grin on her face, so I asked her what she was smiling for and she told me, "You'll see."

We walked down this long corridor that was so damn beautiful. The whole time candy was holding my hand and telling me that she was gonna make the time we spend together something I would never forget. Shit, I was there already.

We went into this purple pink room with ruffles all over. She told me to take a shower so she could talk the details over with my moms, and she'd be ready when I got out. It took me about 10 minutes to shower and I thought I kept hearing moaning. I figured she had a porno on the big ass flat screen in the room. I dried off stepped out of the bathroom and my mouth dropped open. My mother was on her back legs wide open, and Candy was eating her out. I didn't know what to think but my dick got so hard it started to throb. I guess I was standing there too long because Candy got up wiped her mouth and told me to come to the bed. My moms said, "Surprise! I wanted to make this a day to remember, so I got one of my regulars to do us." I told her, "Well I don't know how to respond to that." Before I could say anything else, I felt this hot sensation on my dick, and when I looked down Candy had my whole dick in her mouth. My moms proceeded to eat Candy from behind while Candy sucked my dick at the end of the bed. I started to pre cum all in her mouth, and she stopped in her tracks. She told me, "well, I better stop; we don't want it to end too quickly." She told my moms to lay way back on the bed with her legs open; then she gave me a condom and told me to fuck her from behind while she ate my moms out. She threw my moms legs way back and started humming on her pussy. It made me so excited, I almost dropped the condom. I put the condom on and entered her. The feeling was so intense. Sweet heat surrounded my dick, and she squeezed every time I pulled out. She jerked up her ass every time I went in. Her ass started making clapping noises like I was hitting it with my hand. My moms started making these soft sounds, and she told her to keep it right there. They both started making loud noises, and they both came at the same time. After, Candy told me to hold her waist and fuck her hard, hard as I could. My moms reached under her and started sucking on her tits. Candy started *shaking all over. Her pussy started making squishy sounds and she let out a loud scream. She shot her cum all over my dick and nuts. She jumped up and lay on her back. She told my moms to sit on her face while I fucked her. I held her by her feet and fucked her as hard as I could. My moms sat on her face and had her head back making gurgling noises, and were thrusting her pussy back and forth. Candy started shaking again and again squirted all over me. She moved her head away from my mom's pussy and stuck three of her fingers in her. My moms went bananas. She started screaming, "Oh shit! Oh Shit! I'm ready baby, I'm ready". Candy then reached over and pressed a button. Two minutes later a guy entered the room and went straight for my mother. My mother and Candy lay side by side on the bed as me and this stranger fucked the shit out of them. They leaned towards each other, kissed each other, and fondled their tits. I held my moms right leg and he held Candy's left leg. They told us to slow down because they wanted to cum at the same time. So we took it slow. Sweat started running down my back and I started getting this feeling in between my legs. It was stronger than the feeling I got when I jerked off; more intense. He looked over at me and told me to let Candy know when I was gonna cum. I told him okay and kept fuckin'. My* moms and Candy started moving real fast and jerked back and forth. They started kissing and yelled, "we're cumin: harder, harder." We both put our backs into it, bent their legs al the way back and fucked them like we were doing push ups. Of course I was following him, cause I was to busy enjoying myself. They were jerking and screaming so much we had to really hold them down. They let out this loud scream and started shaking and squirting all over us. It seemed like they came forever. After they calmed down a little, but told us to keep fuckin them. I started to get the feeling that I was gonna cum and I told Candy. Candy jumped up and put my dick in her mouth. She sucked it from the tip of my head to my nuts. The stranger kept fuckin my moms, but they were both watching us. It's kind of exciting fucking and watching somebody else fuck in the same room. Candy was making love to my dick. The feeling in between my legs was so intense. I told Candy I was cumin' and she took the condom off and started suckin me raw dog. Oh my God I was in heaven. The feeling started in my nuts, went to my feet then to my head. I came so hard I thought my head was gonna explode. My dick was down her throat when I came. She didn't even taste it until I was finished cuming. She pulled it out her mouth and kept sucking it. She sucked *all the cum out. Not one drop of cum hit the bed her face, or anywhere else. I shook so much I fell to the bed and totally forgot anyone else was in the room with us. After I calmed down, I looked up and the three of them were looking at me smiling. Moms told the stranger, "thank you for taking time out to help her out." He told her, "for you, anytime." Her kissed her on her cheek and left the room. Candy was standing there with her hand on her pussy. She told moms, "That was the shit! I still feel him in me." They both laughed at that and went to the door. Moms told her to give us a couple minutes, and we'll be right out." Candy agreed and left the room.*

"Well Jeff, what do you think?" I told her, "At first I didn't know what to think, but after I just went with the flow. I wish it lasted longer." She put a card in my hand and told me it was Candy's card and to call when ever I wanted to come."

I guess the hangover is worth it. What do you think?

Old School Crush

I woke up early to check my email. I logged into my cafe-space page. I have a bunch of messages from friends and clients. I noticed I have a friend request. I opened the page and it's a guy with most beautiful eyes I've ever seen requesting to my friend. "Of course we can be friends", I thought to myself. I approved his friendship.

I began to look on his page to see what this guy was all about. I looked into his pictures. I saw that we knew the same people and went to the same Public School. I came across one of his pictures that had a clear visual of his face. "Oh my god, I know this guy!" I said out loud, lucky for me I was home alone. I couldn't believe I found an old school crush online.

I sent him a note explaining to him who I was and that I knew him. Later on that day he wrote back. He said, "Hey Miss, I know you too. How you been? I see you're doing big things now. Keep in touch." It was a very short and to the point note.

I wrote him back answering his questions. This episode went on for a few days. I got up enough nerve to reveal my secret. In the next letter, I wrote and explained to him that I had a major crush on him back in the day. Just by writing this letter I got all hot and bothered. I wanted to rekindle a flame that I never got the chance to light. I was willing to have an affair with him. All I need is one night with him. I poured my heart out in the letter; I prayed hard that he didn't diss me.

I checked my messages later on that night and he answered me back. I was nervous to open it, but I did. Come to find out he felt the same way. He left me his number to call him. I immediately called him. Yes, I was opened!

We talked for awhile and set up a date to meet later on that night. I took out my freak dress & shoes. I wanted to see what he missed out on.

Finally, we met up with each other and it was like

an instant connection. We hugged each other and I kissed him passionately. (I had to bend down a little because he's kind of short) We both knew what time it was. We went to the hotel and it was on and poppin! He fucked me very well! All I can say is big things come in small packages. We went at it for 2 hours straight. I was curious about him anyway and he killed all that.

After our freak session he took me home. I didn't want him to leave, but I had no choice. Just looking at him put me in a spell. His eyes are gorgeous and his eyelashes make them stand out. His sexiness was killing me. I had to get away from him instantly. I kissed him goodnight and got out the car. He waited until I was inside my building before he drove off.

How can someone be so loving and caring now, when in grade school he was a pain in the ass? I'm just glad he grew out of it. He is a real man now. I just wish he could be all mine.

Who would have thought that the opportunity of getting with an old school crush would ever come true?

White Chocolate

I met a guy name John Winston last summer. Just the thought of him makes me moist. I regret not making him mine at the time. I was worried about what my family would think of me dating a white guy. John was white in skin color but had the swagger of a black man. He even had a dick like one and knew how to work it in bed. He use to make me scream out his name. I couldn't get enough of him. He enjoyed eating my pussy; he would do it whenever I wanted him to do it. He made me a sex addict.

My world fell apart when John got a promotion and had to relocate to France. He begged me to come with him, but I couldn't allow myself to go. He proposed to me and I turned him down. I was use to having my white chocolate the way I wanted it. I was having fun and living for the moment marriage would have ruined our lives, so I thought.

Now that he's gone I feel empty inside. I tried to replace my white chocolate for another and it wasn't the same. I immediately ended that fling. Two weeks later I received a letter in the mail from John. He told me that he still wants me and that he would take care of me for the rest of my life. In the envelope was a ticket to France and a number to reach him. I called him and we talked for hours. I accepted his invitation to join him in France. He was very happy and so was I.

A year later

Here I am in France chillin with my white chocolate and my big belly. Yes, I have a little butter cream growing inside of me. We got married a week after I got here. His family adores me and they can't wait for the arrival of their grand child. We see so many mixed couples and we fit right in. I'm so happy I made the right choice. I will never let my white chocolate get away from me ever again!

<u>Girlfriend</u>

If I was your girlfriend.....

Would you tell me all of your deep and darkest secrets?

Would you pour your heart out to me when you feel hurt?

Would you let me take care of you and protect you from harm?

Would you make love to me as if it was the last time we're on earth?

If you had no money, would you let me provide for you?

Would you leave your homies to be with me?

Would you kiss me from head to toe?

I would love to know what's on your mind. If you had to think hard about any of these questions, I guess you're not ready for me to be your girlfriend. Just know that I would do all of these things, If I Was Your Girlfriend!

The Burn

I want it!

I have to have it!

I need it inside me!

Damn I'm on fire!

Is it because I'm high off his loving?

Is it because I miss him so much?

No.. I have the answer, it's called the Burn!

I'm hot for him.

I crave his touch, kisses, and passionate love making.

My soul is on fire.

No water could put out this desire.

It's the Burn!

Private Dancer

(Chapter One)

Being a mother four is not easy; I have two boys and two girls; they mean the world to me. I give them anything they want as long as I can afford it. This summer we went on a cruise for 21 days, we left July 3rd and returned on the 24th. We had a blast! My kids really enjoyed themselves and that made me feel good. To bad we had to come home.

We caught a cab from the airport and arrived home just in time to get things together for their next vacation with their dad. We put our bags and clothes away, cleaned the house, everyone took their showers, ate and went to bed. I had to get up early and go grocery shopping and do laundry. My ex-husband, Omar is coming to pick them up around three-o-clock; he's taking to his family reunion in Baltimore for two weeks and to Florida for another two weeks. I must say he takes good care of his children, he's always there for them in every way possible and I realize that I'm blessed in that department.

(Chapter Two)

My alarm went off at 6:30am, I was still tired but I had a busy day ahead of me. I took a hot shower to wake me up completely. Everything I wear has to match; my color of the day is pink and grey. My sweat suit is grey with pink stripes; I'm wearing my pink and grey air max with my Baby Phat bag to match. As for my hair, I keep it in braids. I don't have time to do it so why bother.

I left a note for my oldest son to get everybody up and make their breakfast. He helps me out a lot, sometimes he reminds me of his father.

I grabbed my shopping cart and headed out the door; I put on my shades and strolled down Carlton Avenue. My neighborhood is quiet and perfect for my family to live. I grew up in that house and my parents left it for me o raise my kids in. Where I live I'm surrounded by shopping malls and grocery stores. My job is not too far from me and my kids schools are near by.

As I walk down Greene Avenue, I think of how much debt I'm in and I need some extra cash to pay of the bills that I accumulated while on vacation. I spent half of my savings, which leaves me at $5,000 in the bank, which I refuse to touch. I started to do a quick budget in my head. After taxes I bring home $1100 bi-weekly, my ex-husband pays me $1200 monthly for child support. I have an $800 mortgage, car payment and insurance of $800, food bill $450, childcare fees $300, Ballet and Karate $400, electricity bill $160, gas bill $80, allowance $220 all monthly payments. I need a second job, something on the weekends, preferably at night. I refuse to let my bills stress me out.

Before I knew it, I'm turning the corner on Hanson Place and walking towards the Atlantic Mall. I love shopping there, I feel so comfortable, it never gets rowdy and all my favorite stores are there. I do all my household shopping at Target, they always have great sales.

My cell phone goes off and of course it's Bryce yelling in my ear, "Mom, where are you? Its 1:00pm and dad just called saying he's on his way to pick us up." "Ok Bryce I'll be home in 20 minutes, keep your shirt on!" I hung up the phone and rushed out the mall; I caught a taxi and headed home. We pulled up in front of the house and I see Omar's BMW. I took all my bags and put them my cart and went inside the house. "Well it took you long *enough!" said Omar. "Kiss my ass!" he started laughing and said, "Let's go to your room and I'll do more than kiss it." I ignored him and went upstairs.*

I went into the boy's room and told them to hurry up; my girls were ready as always, they love traveling. I went in my room and pressed my answering machine. I had one message from my friend Shelby. "Hola Yamia, call me as soon as you get in, we need to talk." I wonder what it is now; sometimes she could be very annoying. I'm in no hurry to call her back; I'm not in the mood to hear her bitching about her relationships, she need to leave the boys alone and get with a real man. I saved her message and went downstairs. My kids were ready to go, I gave them hugs and kisses and off they went with Omar.

(Chapter Three)

I wasn't due back to work until the 31st; I had enough time to take care of my business. I had to make phone calls and get this house back in order. I put on some jazz music, poured a glass of red wine and enjoyed the music. Between the wine and the music, I was relaxed and my mind was blank. I finally had some "me" time, it was long over due.

I went upstairs and turned on the shower, (it's wonderful to have a bathroom in the bedroom.) while the music was playing, I gave my body the ultimate deep cleaning. As the water ran down my back, I opened my legs and started to play with vagina; it felt so good. I started fucking my finger as if it was a dick, (it's been a long time since I had a man to touch me.) my body started to tremble; this intense feeling came over me. I couldn't hold back from moaning, as the feeling grew stronger, I screamed out, "Oh my God!" my sweet juices ran down my leg, I really needed that! I rinsed off and got out; I dried myself off, oiled my body, threw on some old clothes and began to clean my house.

Hours later the phone rings, it's Shelby, "What's up chic? I'm near your house, can I stop by? She asked. "Of course, where are you?" "I'm near target; I'll be there in a half hour." "Ok I'll see you soon." I grabbed the remote and shut off the stereo and turned the T.V. on. I'm twenty minutes into my show and the bell rings. I get up to open the door, because I know its Shelby. She barged in with all these bags from Mandee and Target. "Did the kids leave yet? I bought the girls some clothes and the boys have stuff for their room." "The kids left hours ago." "I wanted to see them before they left again, oh well I guess I'll see them when they get back." "So what do I owe this visit?" I asked. She handed me a flyer which read, "Looking For Beautiful Women To Private Dance", call Mr. Thunder at (800)-1P-DANCE. I looked at her and said, "I'm desperate but that's going too far!" "Oh come on it's nothing! I'm doing it and the money is off the hook! I start tomorrow at 10:00pm, just come and watch me dance, check out the atmosphere, you'll love it." I was lost for words; I never knew she would end up doing some shit like this. "Shelby, how could you let a flyer get the best of you?" "Now you're talking crazy! My sister works there and the money she makes is damn good! She invited me to one of her shows and I like the action and the men treat you like a goddess. I'm only doing this for a couple of months, that's all I need and it's a wrap. Just give it some thought ok."

I sat there for awhile letting it soak in, to see if I could picture myself doing this. "I tell you what; I'll come to your show and check it out, if I like it, I'll let you know but if I feel uncomfortable, I'm leaving your ass there! Do we have a deal?" "I'm cool with that, but you're going to love it!" "Whatever Shelby!"

<u>Meeting Remo</u>

(Chapter Four)

Damn it's boring! The quietness was starting to get to me; I ran upstairs, searched through my closet and pulled out my light blue skirt set. I sprayed my hair and tied it up with my silk scarf. I went to the bathroom to freshen up and the phone rang. I figured it was Shelby bothering me again. I answered it on the third ring, "What Shelby!" "This isn't Shelby! I guess your caller id isn't working huh!" "Remo, is that you?" "Yep! Damn girl, you forgot about me?" "No I didn't look at my caller id and I didn't catch your voice. How are you?" "You were on my mind, so I decided to give you a call." "Oh is that right!" "Yes it is." I walked over to the window and this bastard was parked in front of my house in his fly ass Navigator. I'm like this punk is not slick, I know what he wants. He didn't change a bit.

"Remo, what's up with this surprise visit? Why are you in front of my house?" "I just wanted to see you; I felt it was right to call before I knocked on your door. So, can I come in or are you going to come outside?" "I'm not dressed; I'll come down and open the door." I

threw my robe on and ran downstairs to let him in. A part of me was doing flips inside, because if I was going to be with anyone it would've been him. I kept my cool and let him come inside. He sat on the sofa and I joined him. Instantly my pussy became moist, I knew he was there for sex. I wanted him to fuck me, so I decided to set it off; I gave him a passionate kiss to show him how much I missed him. He opened my robe and started to feel my breast, his hands made its way to my panties. I stopped his hand and demanded him to remove his clothes. I took off my robe and panties; I walked away and went up stairs. He followed me and just I got to the top steps, he swooped me off my feet and carried me to the bedroom. He laid me on the bed; I opened my legs for him to enter me. The sight of his chocolate body and his monstrous dick grove me crazy! He got on his knees and started to taste my sweet pie. I felt as if I was in between worlds, the feeling grew more intense and after a few minutes I exploded in to his mouth. He sucked all my love juices as if he was drinking from a cup. Wow! That was some intense shit! I thought to myself.

He got up from his knees and rammed his monstrous dick inside of me; he banged the shit of my little girl. I felt every inch of his 12 inch dick; I clawed his back with every stroke he gave me. At the moment I didn't care if he had a girlfriend or not, he would have to explain to her about the scratches not me. As he reached his point, he grabbed my breast and began to suck on my nipples. I had to tell him to stop, because he was getting too rough and it began to hurt. He held on to my waist and fucked me harder and harder until I felt his hot cream inside of me, I loved the way his cum felt inside of me.

We both just laid there out of breath, he looked at me and said, "I'm sorry for leaving you, I should've told you why I left." "Don't worry about it; I guess you had your reasons. I'm not mad anymore; I just remember the good times we had. I know we weren't meant to be a couple at that time." "I hear some bitterness in your voice, sounds like you're still mad." "I'm good Remo, I'm not mad at all. Let's forget about it ok." "Ok, I won't mention it again. Well it's time for me to go; I left you a gift on the coffee table." "Where are you headed?" "Now you know I don't want you involved or knowing stuff you don't need to know. I'll keep in touch; I'll take a shower at my place." (I was kind of disappointed, but I knew he wasn't here to stay; I just wished he would stop running from place to place and settle in one spot.)

While he was putting on his clothes, I sat up and just stared at him, I'm concerned and he doesn't even know it. He leaned over, gave me a kiss and left. I didn't have a chance to say anything. I put on my robe and went downstairs to lock the doors, I went in the living room and picked up the envelope and opened it. I couldn't believe my eye; he left money and note along with it. I began to read the letter.

"I know what you're thinking and trust me, I'm doing anything crazy. I always had money and you know that. Here's my voice mail number, call me anytime. I know you got bills and other things to do. $6000 should be enough for now. Just keep in mind that I will always love you, and take care of yourself.)

I didn't know how to feel about the letter, we never had a commitment to each other, so I didn't sweat it. I care about him a lot, if I could chose my husband, it would be him.

Since we met at Shelby's house, we always had a strong attraction to each other. He had his shit together and he took care pf me as well.

I met Remo two years ago at Shelby's card

game. She knows a lot of people from all over. I was chillin, sipping on some Bacardi and coke. When I go out to parties or any gatherings, I put on my best clothes. I was wearing all Coach, my jacket was custom made, the shoes just came out and not many people had them, I sported the watch and hand bag. Nobody in the room could fuck with what I had on, all eyes were on me. I noticed this dark skinned guy clockin me the whole time I was there. I walked over to him and said, "You want something?" in an arrogant tone. "Yeah, I want you! By the way what's your name miss?" "I'm Yamia, but my friends call me Mia. What's yours?" "I'm Ramon, buy my homies call me Remo." I stuck my hand out to shake his hand; he grabbed my hand gently and kisses it. "It's nice to meet you." I said. "Same here."

We sat down next to each other and conversed for a long time, finally we exchanged numbers. I was feeling this guy a lot, he didn't speak ghetto at all and he didn't pretend to be a thug. His friend yelled across the room, "Yo Remo lets be out!" he kissed my hand again and said, "I'll call you tomorrow." "Ok, I'll be home." I replied. As he walked away with his friend, I admired his style; he has a rich taste in clothes. He's bow legged and had a muscular body, I sighed and *went in the kitchen to a soda and some chicken. Everyone was into the game and having a good time. I don't play cards, so I just enjoyed the food.*

Late that night around 1:00am, I helped Shelby clean her apartment. Her phone rang twice before she answered it, "Hello, what's up Remo. She's right here hold on." She walks over to me and gives me the phone. "It's Remo." she whispered. "Hey, what's up? "I just wanted to make sure you were still there, I'm coming upstairs, to finish our conversation. If you don't mind." "No, I don't mind, that sounds cool." "Ok, see you in a minute." "Ok, bye." I gave her back the phone. "Shelby, did you know that Remo was coming back here?" "Yeah, I knew he was coming back with Rocky. I didn't tell you that I'm messing with his home boy." "You little whore! No you didn't tell me, I'm not surprised." "What you mean, you're not surprised!" "Because, you never tell me anything until the last minute, I'm always the last to know." We looked at each other and laughed.

The door opens and it was Remo and Rocky, with Hennessy and Alize in their hands. "Where ya'll at!" they shouted. "Don't you see me right here, what's all the shouting about?"

I responded. "Remo, you got a feisty woman here!" I looked at him and shook my head. "What we got here?" asked Shelby. "Yo Shelby, you gonna make the Hen-Live or what?" Rocky asked. (Hen-live is, Hennessy, Alize, Coca Cola, and a splash of vodka or gin with some crushed ice.) "Yeah, I'm about to do it now." She made the drinks and put them on the table. I grabbed my glass and took a sip; damn it was off the hook! Shelby and Rocky took their glasses to the bedroom and left us (Remo and I) in the living room.

We talked as we sipped on our drinks, I told him about my job and my children. I explained to him that I wasn't looking for a relationship at the moment. He told me about his job at Con Edison and his baby mama drama, he also told me about the job as a transporter. I didn't bother to ask him what he transports, because it's common sense.

After our talk we sat quietly staring into each other eyes. We heard moaning from the bedroom, the sound of Shelby and Rocky going at it made me horny. Remo leaned over and gave a passionate kiss, he was trying to be gentle. I kissed him back, but with more force, that was my way of letting him know that it was ok to be a little rough.

Shortly after our kiss we were fucking each other like dogs in heat, and I was definitely in heat. This brother had it going on, he was more than packing; he was carrying some heavy luggage! Usually when a guy has a big dick he also has small or average balls, this brother had some balls on him and never ending dick. I was heaven, every stroke felt as if he was tarring me a brand new pussy. He sucked my tits like their were candy, he made to my pussy with his mouth and made his way to my ass. He was the first guy to lick my asshole, and that shit felt good!

He took control and sat me on his dick; I rode the shit out of his dick. Our bodies were speaking a language that only we understood, his dick was calling my name. He grabbed my waist and held me on his dick, within a few minutes he exploded. That fuck session hit the spot, damn that was a good fuck!

I couldn't believe that I just fucked a stranger without a condom, which was very stupid thing to do. I got so caught up in the moment that I let my pussy take control over my brain, I just hope it didn't cost me my life.

He looked at the clock and said, "Damn I gotta go, it's 4:00 am and I have to be to work by 7:00. Yo Rocky it's about that time, let's be out!" As he rushing and fixing his clothes, he turns to me and says, "Girl, you got some good pussy! That's my pussy now!" I sucked my teeth and said, "Yeah, ok!" I put on my clothes and pretend as if nothing happened. He walked over to me and gave a roll of money, I was shocked. "What's this for?" I asked. "It's a little something for you, since that's my pussy now; I have to keep your pockets full. Besides that's chump change, I got whole lot more baby." he replied. I kept quiet and put the money in my pocket, I wasn't going to argue about it. I gave him a hug and a sensual kiss; eventually he's going to be mine.

"Aight Remo, let's roll!" said Rocky. They left and I plopped down on the sofa. I waited for Shelby to come out but she never did. I went in her room and she was snoring like a truck driver. I didn't want to wake her, so I put a sticky note on her pillow that read, "Call me tomorrow." I closed her apartment door tightly and flagged me a cab. When I arrived home, I took a shower, put on my t-shirt and fantasized about Remo until I feel asleep.

Every now and then we would have our secret meeting. We would go out for dinner or stay in and fuck all night. He always took care of me and I was spoiled rotten. He gave me anything I wanted and he made sure it was the best. But all the fun had stopped when he disappeared one day, nobody knew where he was, not even his home boy Rocky.

(Chapter Five)

Tonight is Shelby's first night at the club and I promised her I would be there. I took a shower and oiled my body down with honey oil that I purchased from Rosalyn Scent. (Her products are fabulous) I threw on my clothes, sprayed my hair, and I was ready to go. I called Shelby to let her know that I was on my way. I put a couple hundreds in my purse along with my shades. I usually drive when I'm going out, but I didn't feel like taking the car out of the garage, I'll just walk to her house.

Shelby lives in the Clinton Hills Co-op on Waverly and Greene Avenue, her mother and father moved back to Jamaica Queens and left her the Co-op. I must admit she keeps her apartment nice and clean. The neighborhood is quiet and safe. On my way to her house, I stopped Ms. Sandra's shop to by some Rosalyn scent products. I shop there every week, she always has about 10-15 customers purchasing or ordering her stuff. Her skin care products are all natural; the colognes and perfumes are her own creations. I picked up my usual items and paid for them, she always give free samples of what's coming out next. I love shopping there; she is such a wonderful person.

I reached Shelby's building, the outside door was broke and her bell didn't work. I walked up three flights of stairs, (I don't ride elevators) her apartment faces the stair case. I knocked on the door hard enough for her to hear me, she finally opened the door. "Are we going to a wedding that I don't know about?" I said jokingly. "Ha ha very funny Yamia! Go sit down somewhere!" I sat down at the table and waited for her to get ready. "Imencia is on her way, she should be here in 10 minutes." Shelby yelled. "Oh ok, is he working tonight?" "Yeah, that's why she's coming to get us." I didn't reply, I just sat there and waited for her.

Imencia is Shelby's sister, she's a true hustler. For her to be young, she got her head on the right track. She has a good personality but she don't play no games, that chic will get down for hers. Imencia takes care of herself and will let anybody know that she don't need a man to do shit for her, to be honest I don't think there's a man that could afford her. This *is her last year in school, she a manager at Citibank and to keep her pockets fat, she's a dancer on the side. Her apartment is near the Promenade (in Brooklyn) and to top it off, she has a bad ass Benz as well. This chic is definitely living the good life.*

The bell rings and I answered it, "Who is it?" "It's me, come downstairs, I'm double parked!" "Ok, we're coming now." I grabbed my stuff and Shelby came running out like a mad woman, her slow ass takes forever to get ready.

I get in the car and greet Imenia with a smile. "So what's up chic? I see you still ballin, I'm feeling this car!" "I'm just doing me, I don't have any kids and the guys that I fuck with already know what I'm about, this is my last year in college and I'm trying to stay focused." "I hear that! Here comes your super model sister, she's a hot mess!" we chuckled as Shelby got in the car. "What so funny?" Shelby asked. "What the fuck, all white? You're really trying to stand out." "Look Imencia, I don't have time for your sarcasm; anyway, those bitches never wear white! All they wear is hot pink, gold, black and red, those colors are corny!" "You're right, I'm feeling you on that shit!" said Imencia.

I'm chillin in the back seat enjoying the ride to this place called the Hide Out in Long Island City; it's near Queens Bridge projects. I heard Imencia tell Shelby that Mr. Thunder and his friends are having an after party once the show is over. I noticed that we started to slow down; I look to the left and saw this warehouse with expensive cars parked in the parking lot. Imencia parked next to this fly Jaguar. I asked her, "Whose car is that?" she answered, "That's Noemi's car, she fuck with this cat named Adonis." "Damn, that shit is hot! I never saw a hot pink Jag before." "Well, you keep coming here and you'll see cars and trucks that you didn't know they made." We got out the car; Imencia opened her trunk and took out her clothes for tonight's show, Shelby kept her clothes with her. I started to get nervous because this wasn't my scene, I don't go to clubs or hang out in secluded places.

Shelby and Imencia showed their V.I.P passes and I walked in behind them. This place was ugly on the outside but glamorous inside, it looked like a palace. There were beautiful crystal chandeliers all over and a huge stage built like a runway. The chairs and tables were a platinum color with silver glitter fabric over the table. The bar was exotic, it was located in the back of the club; the whole bar design was with platinum color furniture, the drinking glasses were red and the bartenders wore red suits with silver ties and shoes. Everything in this club was extravagant.

I sat at one of the tables to watch my home girls get busy, as I looked around; admiring the set up, there were a lot of women coming in to do their act, most of them were wearing very expensive clothes. These chic's know how to dress, one chic had on a fly light blue Dolce & Gabbana dress with gold trimmings on it, gold pumps with a matching bag. I was really feeling that outfit, that something I would wear.

I saw Shelby and Imencia talking to this big dark skinned guy, wearing a blue suit. He had a thick platinum chain hanging over his shirt. I could tell they were discussing business; just by the way he was expressing himself. Shelby started to walk towards me with a big smile on her face. "Girl I'm so excited! He is paying me $1000 per show that I do tonight." "How many are you performing tonight?" I asked out of curiosity. "I'm doing three stage shows and one V.I.P show." "Damn girl, you really putting in work huh?" "That's right girl!" "So what time are we leaving out of here?" "Well I go on at 8, 10 and 12, Imencia goes on at 9 and 12; she only has two shows tonight." "Ok, well I guess I'll leave after your second show." "Why are you leaving? How are you going to get home?" "Don't worry, I'll take a cab, I do have money you know." "Whatever! You're such a dead ass! I'm glad you came anyway." she gave me a hug. "Girl I gotta go and get ready, wish me luck." "Don't hurt nobody girl, Good luck."

(Chapter Six)

The club started filling up fast; all types of ballers were coming through. These men had money, every guy that walks through those doors wore a Stacy Adams and Armani suits, nothing less than that. I felt as if I was at a fashion show. I noticed the female ushers would greet them at the door and seat them in a certain area of the club; they were wearing spaghetti strap dresses that matched the scenery of the club. An usher walked over to me and said, "Miss, I'm sorry to bother you, but you have to sit at the bar to watch the show." "Oh ok." I replied. I got up and walked over to the bar and sat on those beautiful platinum stools. I was impressed by her politeness. The women were very polite to the men as well.

I was sitting at the bar chillin and observing

my surroundings. I felt a tap on my shoulder, I turned around to see who it was and oh my God it was Remo! My heart started to pump fast and my eyes almost popped out of my head. "What the hell are you doing here?" I asked. I looked him up and down and realized he was wearing the same suit and chain as the owner, then it hit me, this is the same man Shelby and Imencia were talking to. He was looking real good in that suit; I couldn't keep my eyes off of him. "Hey baby, how you're doing?" he asked as he kissed my lips. "I'm fine, now answer my question, what are you doing here?" "To be honest, I own this club, I'm Mr. Thunder. Nobody here knows me as Remo. I do everything else, but hire the women. I have someone to that for me." "Ok Mr. Big Time, so you do know that Shelby and her sister work here right?" "Hell yeah I know about that, but they don't know that I'm their boss and I would like to keep it that way. They think I'm filling in for someone else." "Oh ok, well my lips are sealed." I replied.

I really didn't want to talk to him, but I wanted to ask him why he left. I thought about it for a minute while he looked around the club, finally I got up enough nerve to ask him. "Remo, why did you leave like that? What were you running from and why?

Please be honest with me." "Something's are not for you to know, I don't want you involved in any shit that I do! The less you know the better it is. Trust me; I'm being real with you." "I was worried about you; I didn't know what happened to you. I see your doing well, how long you had this place?" "Not long, maybe a tear if that." "You had this for a year and couldn't let me know what was up with you. I think you are full of shit! I guess ole girl had to keep a tight leash on you huh." "What the fuck you mean? I'm my own boss, nobody tell what the fuck to do, I'm a grown ass man. And just to let you know, I'm not with "ole girl" anymore." "Ok, ok, don't get hype, I'll drop the subject." "Thank you very much!" I could see he was still mad so I wanted to calm him down a bit. "I'm sorry for getting on you like that, so I'll make it up to you; let me buy you a drink." "Nah, that's ok, I'm cool. Let me ask you a question, what are you doing here?" "I'm here to watch my home girls dance and soon as their done, I'm going home." "Is that right, and how are you getting home?" "I'm taking a cab home; I'm a big girl." "No doubt about that." "You should know that I always have a plan A and B, oh I guess you forgot." "Nah, I was just checking, that's all."

He thinks he is so slick, he was trying to find

out if someone was picking me up, I know his little game. He reached over and grabbed my hand and said, "I'm not going to lie to you, I did miss you a lot. I thought about you everyday that went pass, I was at a point where I wanted to come and be with you and the kids, but I couldn't bring ya'll in my shit. If anything was to happen to you or those kids, I would go crazy. I'm being real and this shit is coming from the heart." "I understand and I told you I'm not mad." "So tell me, why are you trying to work here? This shit is not you at all; you're way too classy for this shit." "How did you know if I was thinking about working here?" "I know everything, trust me! Well you put that shit out of your mind, because it ain't going down like that."

I was surprised, because I couldn't figure out how he knew about that, sometimes I just can't figure him out.

(Chapter Seven)

The show was about to start. He said, "Come to my office, we could watch the show from there." "Ok, but don't try to kidnap me!" I said jokingly. We walked down this long corridor that led to his office, we came to a steel door, he pressed four numbers and the door automatically opens.

You could tell he hired a professional to decorate his office; I was amazed that he had such great taste. His office was as big as a one bedroom apartment, as you walk in there was a cherry wood desk and a matching executive chair on the left side of the room. He had huge flat screen television on the wall; on the right side he had plants and a cherry wood dinner table with four chairs around it. I guess that's where he eats his food.

"Wow you have such a beautiful office; I wouldn't expect this from you at all. I must say I'm impressed, it looks like you could live here." "I do live here; I'm not with "ole girl" anymore. I give her money for my daughter and I agreed to pay her rent for a year, after that she's on her own. Let me show you the other room."

He opened another door that led to his other hidden haven. This room was better that the first one, he had a 60 inch television, a full living room set and three monitors on the wall, which was hooked up to a security camera. You could see and hear everything clearly. This man has a rich taste and I loved it; I put my bags down and sat on his loveseat. He took of his jacket and sat next to me. I couldn't believe I was watching the

*show from his office, this had me trippin out.
"How much do you charge to enter the club?"
I asked. "Well that depends on where they sit
and if they have any special request." "Do
you mind explaining it to me in detail,
because I don't understand?" "Ok this how it
goes, the men that come here are regulars,
some sit on the platinum side and the others
usually sit at the gold side. The platinum area
is for the big ballers, they drop $400-$600 for
a private dance and a V.I.P special. The gold
side area is for the small timers, they pay
$100-$300 for a private dance. The V.I.P
spots are for the guys that just come here to
fuck and do whatever; they don't care about
getting a dance. That's where the real money
comes in at, two hours id $400 and four
hours is $800. Some nights it gets so packed
in here that we have to break down the shows
and that's when we close at 6:00 am. I get be
paid lovely!" "Damn boy you know how to
make some money!" "I do what I gotta do! I
don't let in anybody from the projects
because they always cause drama and they
don't peel off money like my members do. My
members are doctors, lawyers, stock brokers
and sometimes judges roll up in here, and
they got money to burn. These girls have to
make a living for their families; some of them
don't have a high school diploma or a GED
and can't get a regular 9 to 5. I'm just making*

a way for everybody to eat." "I'm impressed!" "The show is starting, would you like a drink Yami?" "Sure, do you have any Hen-Live?" "I have it right here baby." He gave me a glass filled to the top, he turned the lights down and we watched the show.

(Chapter Eight)

The host came out and announced who was coming out, the music came on and this chic name Luxury came out. She was wearing a costume made out of diamonds, her earrings, necklace, ring, bracelet and anklet were diamonds. Her performance was very classy and smooth, she dance to her theme song which is Luxurious by G. Stephanie. She did her routine near the platinum side. This tall guy walked on stage with a hand full of money in his hand. She did a split and rolled on her back, her legs were spread open; the guy bent down and began to eat her pussy. After a minute or so, he stopped and put the money in her thigh string and walked away wiping his mouth. The crow went crazy; I could imagine every man with a hard dick right about now. Luxury finished her routine, as her performance was coming to an end; she picked up the money off the floor, blew a kiss to the crowd and walked off the stage.

My girl Shelby was up next, her theme song was "Rock the Boat". My girl was rockin that body paint, with a white thigh string. She put on a show; she had men from both sides of the club throwing her money. I was proud of her. She had so much money on stage that her sister had to come out and help her collect it.

I was starting to feel nice form the liquor and to be honest; I was hoping that he would start to get a little fresh with me. He must've read my mind, because he touched my knee and moved his hands up to my thigh. I wanted him so bad, that I opened my legs to make it easier for him. As he touched my love box, I felt a warm tingle move through my body; I was definitely ready for him to fuck me.

He began to finger pop me; all of my sweet juices were running down his fingers. My pussy started to squeeze his fingers; I couldn't take it any longer. I whispered in his ear, "I need you, my pussy wants you." He looked at me with fire in his eyes. We stripped down to our naked bodies; my inner thighs were soaked from my sweet juices. He dropped his pants and that chocolate dick stood at straight out. My eyes were glued to it, I grabbed it and gave it a good squeeze, and a huge amount of pre cum came oozing out.

We attacked each other like wild animals, we fucked for hours. We gave each other oral sex; I sucked his like a lollipop. I concentrated more on the tip of his dick and within seconds he exploded in my mouth and I swallowed every drop of his butter cream. I could suck his dick all night, that's how much I enjoy doing it.

Hours passed and we were tired from all the fucking and sucking. We laid there holding each other, I missed being with him but he lives a lifestyle that I can't commit to. He whispered in my ear, "I missed you so much, if I was ready to give up all this, I would marry you right now!" "That's nice to know, but things happen for a reason and time has its own way of taking place. It's getting late and I have to go home, but before I go I have a surprise for you!" "Oh yeah, what you got for me?" I walked over to the stereo and pressed play, I didn't know what was in there, I just took a chance. It started to play a song called, "Read your Mind". He sat up and gave me his full attention, as the music blast from the speakers; I started to dance in front of him. I rolled my body back and forth; I moved closer to him and began to grind on him. I backed away and finger fuck myself to the rhythm of the song. I made myself cum; I came so hard that I squirted onto the floor. I revealed a side of me that he'll never forget.

(Chapter Nine)

My cell phone went off; I looked at my screen to see who was calling me, it was Shelby. I answered the phone. "Hello Shelby." "Don't hello Shelby me! Where are you?" "Give me a few minutes, I'll be out." I hung up the phone before she could ask me anymore questions. I turned to Remo and said, "Baby I got to go, Shelby just called." "I thought you were taking a cab." "Yeah, that's what I thought, but since I didn't leave like I was suppose to, I'll just leave with her." "Damn baby I thought you were staying with me tonight, I want us to spend some time together." "I don't mind being with you, but she's waiting on me. What am I going to tell her?" "Tell her you're with me." I looked at him and smiled. I called Shelby back. "Hey Shelby, I'm not going home right now, I'm going to chill with Remo for awhile." "I knew he was going to spot your ass, I know you fucked him! You better give me details tomorrow." "I promise I will, I'll talk to you later.

If I didn't hang up on her, she would've kept me on the phone all night. I wanted to spend all my time with Remo, not on the damn phone with her.

"So, what are we doing to do tonight?" I asked. "I just want to spend some time with you. In a couple of weeks I'll be out of town. I have some shit to take care." "Damn Remo, when are you going to leave that lifestyle alone, you're not getting any younger, don't you want to live a settled life?" "I hear what you saying and I do have plans to settle down, but I got to take care of this shit before I move on. You know your friend is going to ask you about me?" "Why would she do that?" "Because she is still worried about Rocky, and that motherfucker is dead!" "What you mean dead?" "He is no longer living, that's what I mean." "Does Shelby know?" "Nah, she don't know yet, she'll find out later." "Who killed him?" "Those Greek guys from Astoria. He kept fucking with their money and not paying it back, and on top of that he was smoking crack. I had to leave that nigga alone." "Wow, I didn't know he was smoking crack, damn that's some crazy shit. Did Shelby know what he was doing?" "Hell yeah she knew! She was doing it with him for awhile and sniffing coke, she didn't tell you?" "Oh my God, she never told me anything about that at all, I can't believe what I'm hearing." "Well believe it, she's one of those functional drug addicts." "Damn, that's some

serious shit! I would've never known about this if you didn't tell me." "Just be careful around her, don't go to every card game or party she throws, because home girl gets down and dirty with it! Trust me, I seen her in action." "I'm good; you know I don't hang out much anyway." "Keep it that way; I don't want anything to happen to you."

I was in so much shock, what I just heard couldn't be true but I know he wouldn't lie to me. He never did so far, so why start now. That shit with Rocky blew my mind completely. If she doesn't know what happened to him, that's on her because I'm not getting involved, I refuse to be in the middle of some crazy shit and jeopardize my family! That goes to show, that you don't know people as well as you think you do.

(Chapter Ten)

Here I am laying next to a man that I wanted to be in my life; I knew it would never happen because of his dangerous lifestyle. As I'm watching him sleep, I start to admire his looks, damn he's fucking gorgeous! I love his chocolate skin tone and full lips; he's every woman's dream and more. The thoughts of being married to him and carrying his child played in my mind, so much for wishful thinking.

We slept on the pull out couch, the mattress wasn't like your ordinary couch mattress, this mattress was thick and soft. My body sunk into the mattress and instantly I was knocked out.

I turned over to wrap my arms around my chocolate candy bar and he was gone. I thought I was dreaming, I got out of bed and looked in the other room. He was gone for sure, I went in the bathroom and there was a pink robe with a towel, wash cloth, toothbrush, perfume and a rose on top of the sink. Everything was laid out so neat and pretty, this was very nice of him to do.

Since it was already morning, I turned on the shower and got in; the water felt so good hitting against my body. I lathered up and scrubbed my skin; I did everything I need to do and got out. I opened the bathroom door and went back to the room. I couldn't believe my eyes, he made the bed, laid my moisturizers on the pillows and a full breakfast was waiting for me. I smiled because; I never in my life came across a guy that took care of me in such a way. I didn't think men were capable of doing nice things for woman without having some strings attached to it.

"Hey baby, how did you sleep?" "Oh boy, I slept like a baby. I see you out did yourself this morning?" "You should know by now that I'll do anything for you. While you're eating, I'm going to oil you down and when you're done eating, where going shopping." "What are we shopping for?" "Whatever you want to buy, it's all about you baby. I also want to make sure you have everything you need before I leave again." "Ok, I'm cool with that and you know I love to shop!" He smiled. I wasn't going to turn down a shopping spree; I ate my food while he oiled my body. I see he went in my bag and used my stuff, but that's ok, he could do that.

I finished my breakfast and put on my clothes. Remo was sportin some fly ass True Religion jeans with a bright white t-shirt and a pair of white air max. I've known Remo for quite awhile and I never seen him dress sloppy, he always dressed fly. He's a man with style.

"Are you ready princess?" "Yeah I'm ready, so where are we headed?" "We're going to New Jersey, I hate shopping here because you'll see the so many people with the same

outfit on, I like to be different, you feel me?" I nodded my head in agreement. We went through this back door that led to his garage. He had a bad black Navigator, detailed in gold. The rims on the truck were gold also. He opened the door like a gentleman, the truck smelled clean and sweet. His truck was fully loaded and had some customized work done to it as well. I love a man with style and class. He got in and started the truck, the garage door opened and we were facing the highway. The sun was beaming in my face; I reached in my bag and pulled out my Coach sunglasses. He plugged his Ipod and the music came roaring out from the speakers. I enjoyed the smooth ride to New Jersey.

Sometimes I wonder what's going on in his head. I know he can't be 100% happy about the way he lives; it's not natural to live in suspense or discomfort all the time, I couldn't live like that. I think that's why he's not with his baby mama; I guess she couldn't deal with the stress and not knowing what he was doing out there. If that's the case, well I don't blame her. She has to think about herself and the baby's safety. I wouldn't want to put my family in danger either. If Remo and I were to be together, he would definitely have to get out the game.

(Chapter Eleven)

I felt his hands touch my face; I woke up to his bright white teeth smiling at me. "Hey baby, we're here. You were knocked out on me." "Oh baby, I'm so sorry, I guess the smooth ride relaxed me a little too much." "That's cool baby, don't worry about it. Are you ready to tear the mall up?" "Hell yeah, let's do this!"

We walked in the mall and I was so excited, I finally got the chance to be with him in an open place where we could hold hands and play the role of husband and wife. We couldn't do this in Brooklyn without someone seeing us and spreading gossip. He always treated me like a queen and I loved it. We had a connection with each other that was indescribable at times. I also know that the story he told me about Rocky has some truth to it, but he was still hiding something. Time will tell and things will come out, I'll jus wait for it. I'm not going to start talking about it again and ruin my shopping trip; oh no I can't do that.

"What stores are we going to hit up first?" I asked. "Any store you want, don't worry about the money or the prices, I got that!" "Oh so you got it like that huh?" "That's right

baby, I got it like that!" "Well on that note, let's get it on baby!" I replied.

We shopped in every store there was, I bought my kids some clothes and sneakers. I got so much stuff for myself, it was crazy! By the time we were completely finished, we had to get the security guards to help us take the bags to the truck. The back seats were filled. I felt like a spoiled brat, I liked that feeling. I never would've shopped like that if I were spending my own money. I have too many bills to be carrying on like that, but this is his money and I was glad to help him spend it. I had a wonderful time.

We pulled up in front of my house. I got out the truck and opened the door to my house. He brought all the bags inside and sat them in the living room. "That's everything, I had a nice time with you baby girl. Thanks for spending time with me." "You're welcome, besides I didn't have anything else to do." "Oh really! Oh ok, interesting!" We stood their laughing for a moment. I realized this may be the last time I will see him again, sadness began to settle inside. "Well baby girl it's that time, I have to go and take of some business and get ready to leave town. I'm not going to call you for awhile, don't worry I'll be careful." "I hope so, I care about you. Please be careful!" "I will baby!" he gave me a kiss on my forehead; he reached in his pocket and pulled out two fat rolls of money. He sat it on my coffee table and left. I was sad to see him go; I just wish he wasn't so fucking hard headed. Even though I'm sad, but I have a strange feeling that this isn't the last time I'm going to see him. I hope my instincts are right.

I flopped on my loveseat and unrolled the money he left on the table, I counted $3000 from one roll and $2500 form the other. I notice when I unrolled the second stack of money a note fell out of it. It read, "I know I told you Rock is dead, but he's not! There's a hit out on him that I have to fulfill, please don't tell Shelby! He did some foul shit and he has to pay! Burn this letter after you read it! When I return, we're going to get married!"

The Shit Hit's the Fan

(Chapter Twelve)

I took the letter and burned it, just like he said. I wasn't getting involved in this shit at all! I9'll give her a call later on, when I finish putting my clothes away.

All the money that Remo has given me over a period of time was put in a safe. I didn't put in my account; I didn't want anyone to question me about adding huge amounts of funds to the account frequently. Banks could get very nosey at times.

I cleared my mind and kept doing what I was doing. I took the bags upstairs and put the clothes away, my kids have enough clothes and shoes to last them for awhile. I had so much designer stuff that it was obscene.

I checked my messages and of course bill collectors were stalking me again. My kids called and left me a message also; I'll call them later on. Omar gets very crazy when I call to check up on them, he's always been crazy, that's why we're not together anymore. I couldn't take his arrogant and controlling ways; I just couldn't deal with it!

Usually Shelby would've blown up my answering machine or my cell phone, but she didn't. I called her and her voice mail came on instantly. "Hey this is Shelby, leave a message!" "It's me Shelby, call me back." I always leave short messages, I hate talking to a voice mail. It wasn't even a split second before she called me back.

"What's up girl?" I answered. "I need to talk to you about Rocky! Something bad is going on and I don't know what to do!" "Ok calm down, what's going?" "This morning I got a call from Rocky saying that Remo set him up and he is hurt badly. He wants me to meet him at the Promenade. I don't know what the fuck to do! I don't trust him." "I thought you and him were tight, what's up with you guys?" "I'm going to tell you everything Yamia because you deserve to know. I knew Rocky for a long time; we were fucking around for a year. We were in a deep relationship; until I found out he had a girlfriend with a baby. I cut off the relationship and just kept him as a friend, I use to let him stash money and drugs in my apartment.

One day I was home and I kept getting harassing calls from his girlfriend. I was already stressed out because my bills were piling up and he wasn't paying me to stash his shit in my apartment. I went his stash and took some of it to pay my bills and the rent, I also sniffed some of the cocaine and it became a habit. Later on that day, I was suppose to meet my sister and have lunch. I figured it was early in the day, so I decided to sniff some coke. I got so high that I passed out; when I woke up I was in the hospital; that's why I didn't come to work for those three days. My family knew about it and I begged them not to tell you because I knew you would be mad at me. When he came to visit me in the hospital, I told him that he could stash his shit in my apartment anymore. He got mad and walked out. I was released the next day, when I got home his stuff was gone and I changed the locks on my door. I remember clearly, when Remo disappeared so did Rocky. Something is not right!" "I don't know what to say about all this madness but I know one thing, I'm not stressing it."

I had to think of something quick, because she could be in danger. I think Rocky or his girlfriend might kill Shelby, I'll strike up another conversation just to see how much information she'll come up with about Rocky.

"Why did you wait so long to tell me this Shelby? I have always been there for you, we talk about everything. As for Reno is concerned; I haven't seen him since the show. He dropped me off at home and that was it, he didn't mention nothing about Rocky or anything else." "I know I should've told you and like I said, I was scared to tell you. I'm sorry." "It's cool. Don't worry about it. I don't think you should meet Rocky; I have a strange feeling he might hurt you. Why don't *you come over to my house and spend the night, I don't want you to be there if he comes looking for you. We could make it a girl's night out, like old times." "Ok, I'll get my stuff and lock up the house. Oh guess what girl, I got a new SUV! It's a Chevy Suburban; we could go out for a ride tonight." "Oh shit, that's what's up! You rollin with the big girls huh?, well hurry up and get over so we could go hang out!" "Ok, I'll be there in an hour, see you then."*

All I could do is think about this madness, I hate being caught in bullshit. My life was simple and quiet before I started fucking with Remo; I guess I caught up in his web. I need to focus on my kids; I'm thinking about taking a leave of absence and get my life in order. I need to spend more time with the kids. I always had thoughts of opening my own business, I could open a boutique that sells handbags, hats, scarves and expensive perfumes, I could work with that. A high class strip club sounds good too, with all this money I have in the safe, I could get something going. Oh well those are just thoughts and maybe one day they'll come true. After this shit, I'm going to need another vacation.

I hear a car outside of my house, I go to the

window and peep out from behind my curtain. I see Rocky getting out the car with another guy. "What the fuck!" I said out loud. I ran up stairs and called Shelby, her phone rings twice and she answered it. "Hey girl, I'm on my way." "No Shelby don't come here, Rocky is outside my house with some guy. I think we should meet at Atlantic Mall, just wait for me inside Target by the second floor elevator. I'll handle what's going on over here; whatever you do don't use your cell phone." "Ok, I'll be waiting for you, be careful and don't do anything stupid! This is bullshit!" "Yeah, I know but what else could we do? I gotta go, I'll see you there." "Ok bye."

The bell ringed, I ran downstairs to answer it. I grabbed my bag to seem like I was already going out. I opened the door and Rocky was standing there with a sly smirk on her face, the other guy face looked hard as stone. "Hey Yamia it's been a long time since I've seen you. How are you?" "I'm fine, what's up? "I just want to ask you something about Remo, can we come in?" "Well as you can see, I'm on my way out and I don't have that much time to talk." I rushed out the door and double locked it. I have a remote alarm on my keychain that secures the house. "Ok, I'm not going to keep you, have you seen him lately?"

"I haven't seen him since the both of you disappeared. When you talk to him, tell him I said I hope he got enough ass that night, because he would never get it again!" "Wow, that's a little too much info and besides Remo and I don't talk, so doubt that he'll get your message! If you happen to hear from him or see him again, tell him that he's a wanted man. Have a nice day." "Whatever, you do the same." they got in the car and drove off. I walked to the Atlantic mall; I went up side streets just in case I was being followed. What I'm going through is something you'll in the movies.

I reached the mall; I took the escalator to the second floor and walked to the back where the elevators were. I saw her standing there biting her nails, she looked so pale and scared. She spotted me and began to walk towards me; she ran the rest of the way and gave me a hug. I knew she was scared out of her mind, I know I was. "Girl I was worried about you, you have no idea how scared I am! " I can imagine, where's your car?" "It's in the garage on the top floor." "Come on let's get out of here."

(Chapter Thirteen)

We reached her SUV; her ride was fly ass hell.

She had it all tricked out. "Damn this shit is hot! I'm feeling this, I taught you well." I said jokingly. "Oh yeah, I learned from the best. I wanted to buy myself something nice, I think I deserve it." "Of course you do, you worked hard for it! When you start having kids; you'll be lucky if you could get a bra out the deal." We burst into laughter, because she knows what I go through with my kids.

I felt like a celebrity, while driving her car. "Where are we headed Yamia?" "I'm taking you to the Westin Hotel." "Where's that?" "In the city." "You know it's going to be expensive." "I don't care right now Shelby; I'm trying to keep you safe." "Wow, you must really love me Mia Mia!" "Knock it off Shelby, you don't have the sense God gave you! You're blessed to have a friend like me, let the church say Amen!" Amen! We both shouted. We turned up the music and jammed all the way to the city.

By the time we reached 42nd Street, Shelby was knocked out. I drove around trying to find to find a nice hotel for us to stay in. I turned down 43rd Street and came across this beautiful hotel called the Westin. I parked the truck in front of the hotel; I tapped Shelby on the arm. "Hey Shelby, wake up! I'm going in to find out if they have any rooms; I'll be back

in a minute." "Ok Mia, I'll wait for you here."
I got out the truck and went in to see what
they had available. The doorman greeted me
as I walked in, "Welcome to the Grand Westin
Hotel." I smiled as I walked pass and headed
for the service desk, I spoke to a young lady
behind the desk. "Welcome to the Grand
Westin Hotel, how may I help you today?" Hi,
I would like to book a reservation starting
today. "Ok let me see what we have available.
We have a suite available, how long are you
staying?" "My sister and I will be here for two
days." "May I have your identification, how
are you paying?" I'm paying with cash." I
handed her my ID. "Will you be using our
parking lot service?" "Yes I will." "Ok, your
total is $950, we serve breakfast and lunch;
we have a gym, spa, hair salon and a few
department stores on the 10th floor. You have
an all access pass to the cafeteria and movie
room. Your suite has two bedrooms, full
bathroom and small kitchen area. Here is
your key and booklets, thanks for staying at
the Grand Westin hotel, have a great day."

I can't believe I just paid $950 for two days,
well what do you expect from a place like this.
I'll just take it as a second vacation. I put my
ID back in my bag and went back to get
Shelby. She was still knocked out; I tapped on
the window and motioned for her to get out of

the truck. A guy in wearing red and white came over to me, "Hello, I'm here to park your vehicle in the lot." "Oh ok, just gives us a minute." Shelby finally got out of the truck, I gave the valet driver the keys and gave me a receipt with the truck parking space number on it. "Anytime you want to go out, call the number on the receipt and I'll bring it out front for you. Enjoy your stay." "Ok, thanks." I gave him a $30 tip and we went in the hotel.

"Wow, this is a beautiful hotel Mia!" "Yeah, I could definitely get use this, when I was checking us in, the lady was telling me about the spas and stores on the 10th floor. I think we should check it out before we leave." "That sounds cool, I think we should go check out our suite and go shopping at Macy's. "Shelby, I was thinking the same thing, let's do it!"

We went to the suite looked around and admired everything, picked our rooms and left. We shopped at Macy's; we ate dinner at the Olive Garden. We spent the whole entire day shopping up and down Manhattan. I must admit, I loved every moment of it and so did Shelby.

We finally went back to the hotel; we we're exhausted from all the walking. I put all my stuff in my room and went back to the living *room area. Shelby was on her phone talking loud and cursing worst than a sailor. I sat down and waited for her to finish. She turned around and saw me sitting there; she covered the phone and whispered, "It's my sister!" I whispered back, "Ok." She stayed on the phone for another 10 minutes; she closed her phone and plopped on the chair. "What's up with your sister, is she ok?" "Yeah, she fine, she was telling me that the club is closed down and Rocky is in a coma." "What! What the fuck happened, do she know who did it?" "No, she said a friend of hers called and told her this morning, they also found a body burnt up in the back room. I don't know how to say this but I think that was Remo's body. I'm not sure, but who else could it be?" "Damn, that's fucked up!" I played it off as if I was sad. I know that's not Remo, but I can't let her know that.*

"I don't know what'd going Shelby, I had no idea that Remo was into anything else other than his job at Con Edison." "Mia, you didn't know he was into drug trafficking? I thought he would have told you that." "Nah, he didn't tell me shit like that, we wasn't in any relationship. We were only fuck buddies, that's it." "So what are we going to do now that Rocky is in the hospital?" "These rooms are paid for two days; we're staying here

until then. Besides, you don't know who might come around looking for you and start asking questions about ya'll relationship. We're gonna keep things as planned and deal with everything else later."

We turned on the T.V. and the news was on. Maria Costa from the channel 12 news was talking about the incident at the club. "An unidentified man was found in the back room of this club around 7am, another guy that was found badly wounded named Rodney Phillips aka Rocky, who is now in a coma at L.I.C. hospital. His wife of 7 years has a comment." I never saw any sign of him being in trouble, he was a loving husband and father. We have three beautiful children, how am I going to explain this to them? How could someone do this to our family." she said while sobbing.

After looking at this shit on the news I didn't know how to feel, Shelby looked sad but there was more anger in her eyes instead sadness. I think she's up to something.

"Shelby, I'm going to take a shower and go to bed, try and get some rest ok." "I will, don't worry I'll be fine." I went in the room, got my towel and took a hot shower.

(Chapter Fourteen)

That shower hit the spot, I felt rejuvenated. I went in my room, put on my t-shirt and got in bed. Before I could drift off to sleep, my cell phone started ringing. I looked to see who was calling me and it's Imencia; immediately I answered the phone. "Hey girl, what's up?" "I'm just calling you with the update about Rocky, he died tonight. The doctor found him with his breathing cord cut and three fingers cut off as well. "Are you fucking serious?" "Yes girl!" "Did they find out who the burnt up man was?" "I heard that the body was identified as a homeless man. The cameras in the club didn't have anything on them, so this whole thing is still a mystery." "That's fucked up! What's going to happen to those girls that worked there?" "Oh please, those bitches don't have shit going for themselves. I saw a few of them working the strip in the back streets near the Queens Bridge. They'll do anything for money. I ain't gonna front Mia, the money was good, but I have a job with a fat ass bank account. My pockets are not hurting, you feel me?" "I feel you, so do you want me to tell Shelby about Rocky or just wait until tomorrow?" "Tell her tomorrow, I don't want her calling me and asking a thousand fucking questions. I'm sorry I called so late, I just wanted to let you know what was going on." "No problem, thanks for calling. If I hear anything I'll let you know." "Ok, good night Mia." "Good night." as soon as my head hit the pillow, I was out like a light! I needed all the sleep I could get.

I turned over and looked at the clock on the dresser, it was 1:00pm, I must've been really tired. I wonder why Shelby didn't wake me up, I never slept this late. I got out of bed and walked into the living room, she wasn't there. I walked to her bedroom and opened the door, she wasn't there either. I started to get worried; I called her cell phone and it went straight to voicemail. I went back to my room; I washed up and put on my clothes. My cell phone goes off and it's Imencia. "Hello.' "Hey Mia, you know your girl snuck out on you last night!" "I realized that when I got up and that was a half hour ago. Where is she?" "I took her to my parent's house, she's out of control!" "What she's doing there and how she's out of control?" "She went to Rocky's wife house and started a big ass fat over there. I didn't know about it until my friend Daisy called me, she told me to come and get Shelby from over there." "You lucky Daisy was there, because they probably would've did her dirty." "Exactly! And not only that Phressia and Phansy are sisters, so you know *they gonna stick together." "You right about that shit! Where's her truck?" "I don't know, she didn't have it when I picked her up. It should be with you." "It's still in the garage then, I'm gonna bring it to your parents house and the rest of her clothes she left. I'll talk to you later." "Ok, bye."*

This chic is really bugging out! I knew she was up to some bullshit. I packed all my things and grabbed the bags she left. I called the valet office, so he could bring the truck in front. I called the service desk and checked out. I finally got downstairs; I gave the key back and went to the truck. I put everything in the back seat and headed to Jamaica Queens.

The traffic was light and I reached Shelby's parents house fast, I parked in front of the Co-ops on Parsons and 89th Avenue. I called Shelby's mom and told her to tell Shelby I was downstairs. Within five minutes, I see her coming out the building looking like a hot mess. I got out the truck to greet her, "Hey Shelby." I said with an attitude. "Hi Mia, I'm sorry that I left and didn't call you. I was going through something and I needed space." "Oh so you call going over to Phancy house and starting trouble with her, needing space? What the is up with you Shelby? You need to snap out of your little funk, you act like he was your husband and shit! This ain't you Shell!" "Look Mia, you have no idea what I'm feeling right now! Yeah, you're right I shouldn't have went over there acting a fool. I was got high and lost my mind. I'm glad I have you as a friend, but I need to handle this on my own. I'm going to be here with my parents for awhile, I'll call you." "Ok, no problem Shell. Take care of yourself, I'll call you when the kids come back home." "Ok, Mia thank you for being there for me, I appreciate it." "Hey, what are sisters for!" I gave her a hug, took my bags out the truck and walked away.

(Chapter Fifteen)

It took me an hour to get home; I had a lot of mail. My neighbor was coming out of her house; she greeted me with a hello like she always does. "How are you today sweetie?" "I'm ok, how are you?" "I'll live; I have a package for you. Its in my hallway, I'll get it for yah. I don't remember ordering anything; I wonder what it could be. She returned with a medium box. "Here you go; it came a couple days ago. Oh and before I forget a young man ask me to give you this envelope, he was tall, dark shinned fellow with a nice body." We broke into laughter; I knew exactly who she *was describing. "Ok Mrs. Bryan thanks a lot for keeping the packages for me." "Oh, it's no problem! How are the kids?" They're doing great. They're on vacation with their dad for the rest of the summer. How's Mr. Bryan and the rest of the family?" "Everyone is doing fine dear. Chauncey is finally giving us grand kids, his wife is expecting twins; I'm so excited! I'm going to spoil them rotten." I hear yah, well tell everyone I said hello and you have a good day Mrs. Bryan." "Ok dear, you do the same." She walked away and I went in my house. I was anxious to read the letter; I wanted to know what he had to say.*

Dear Yamia,

I know you probably still mad at me and that's cool, I just wanted to let you know that I'm ok. A lot of shit went down that I had to handle. I'm sorry for lying to you, but I rather lie than put you and the kids in harms way. I sent you a package, I hope you take care of business and start a new life. I'm not coming back to New York right now.

Well, I have to keep it moving. Take care of yourself and kiss the kids for me. Don't worry I will see you again.

Remo

Reading that letter had me kind of fucked up, because I thought he was going to get his shit together, I guess some people will never change. I opened the box to see what was in it; there was a teddy bear and a jewelry box from Tiffany's. I opened the jewelry box and my mouth dropped, he bought me a diamond and ruby tennis bracelet with matching earrings and necklace. I know he paid out the ass for that shit. Tears rushed to my eyes, I started to fan my face. On the teddy bear was a note pinned to it. I opened the note and the words "OPEN ME" were in big letters. I turned the teddy near over and unzipped the back of the bear. Inside the bear were rolls of money rolled up with rubber bands. There were a total of six rolls of money in the bear, I opened the money and counted fifty 100 dollar bills in each roll.

What person would think of stuffing a teddy with so much cash? I took the money and went up stairs to my room, I gathered all the money that was in my safe and laid it out on my bed. I counted it twice and got a grand total of sixty thousands dollars. I got a pen and wrote down my ideas for my business. The idea of a spa and lounge hit me like a ton of bricks. I think it's time to make that move.

I put all the money back in the safe; I sat at my desk and wrote checks. I paid my car note off and the insurance is paid up for two years. I put money away for my children and I'm starting off debt free. The person I have to thank for all this is not here. I would've love to show him my appreciation, but in due time I will have that chance.

(Chapter Sixteen)

I had meeting with the banks about my loan, the good news is I got it! I finally got my business loan, I waited for this moment for so long and it's here. I deposited all the money that was in my safe into my savings account, everything is coming together like it should be. I know my parents watching over me in heaven. They are my greatest inspiration.

I signed the documents for the spa, it'll be open in October and the lounge will be opening in September. I have a lot of work to do, I hired a designer to design the spa and lounge. I already hired some people to work for me. I tried to get in touch with Shelby, but she hasn't returned any of my phone calls. It would've been nice to have her by my side.

My cell phone goes off, it's a blocked number.

*I took the chance and answered it, "Hello."
"Hey baby girl, what's up?" Oh my God, I
can't believe he called me after all this time.
"I'm fine. How are you doing stranger?" "I'm
good, open the door for me baby." I dropped
my phone and ran downstairs; I opened the
door and my chocolate candy bar was
standing there looking good and better than
before. He got so much bigger and he had
long braids now, he came inside. He touched
my face and kissed me on the lips; he picked
me up and carried me to my bedroom.*

*We went at it for hours! We did everything
you can imagine, our bodies made sweet
music together. The sweat from his body was
sweet but salty, my body was happy to have
him. We took a shower together and laid
around the house cuddling each other. He
touched my hand and said, "Baby. I have
something I want to say." I sat up and
became attentive.*

*"I enjoyed our time together and you were
always there when I needed you. I want you
to know that I'm ready to settle down, I want
to marry you, I want you to have my baby, I
need you in my life. Will you marry Yamia?"
he said with tears in his eyes. "Oh Remo, you
don't know how long I was waiting for this
moment. Yes I'll marry you! I would love to*

be your wife." We embraced each other as the tears of joy fell from our eyes. This is the moment I've been waiting for.

Later on that night I explained my plans to Remo over dinner. He seemed very excited and he helped me with a lot of other things, such as clients. I was happy for once in my life, I have never been with a man that was passionate about business and money, I could see us being a powerful money making couple.

I'm tired of having a boss; it was time for me to be my own damn boss! I want people to work for me; the people I hired for the spa are well educated women and men with a lot of class. I don't have time to deal with ghetto fabulous chic's and their ghetto mentality. I'm trying to build a good reputation for my businesses. I'm the head bitch in charge!

(Chapter Seventeen)

Damn things are turning out better than I thought! Got to get rid of the jitters, after all I'm not the one stripping or giving lap dances. Guess I'll go check on everyone to make sure everything is going right. As I walk through, I'm thinking to myself, "Wow, I finally did it! I got my own business and it's rolling in dough! It's been a hard road but I'm here. I'm going to make this the most popular club in the city. My shit is so unique! Gotta love it! Who would ever think it's also a strip club. I have my lounge up front for a calm atmosphere and the back is something total different. The strippers are doing their thing (men and women). I also have two big rooms in the basement for those private dances, and whatever your money pays for.

Keep in mind that I now have all of Remo's customers plus mew ones. Since this is my club, I'll have to bless my customers with a dance. I grabbed the mic, "Hello, may I have your attention please! I would like to thank all of you for coming out and showing me love, I hope to keep you as regulars. I would like to show my appreciation by dancing for ya'll tonight!" The crowd went crazy! Remo sat at the bar looking like he saw a ghost. The D.J. played Sensual Eruption, I remember the first time I heard that song; I lost my mother fucking mind! I was feelin it since day one.

I showed my ass on stage! Everyone was going wild! My adrenaline was high! I had to show my customers that I could get down like the rest of the dancers, shit nobody couldn't tell me nothing.

Remo was delighted to see me dance, because he knew when we got home, I was going to give him his special private dance. I'm his business partner, wife, and private dancer.

www.ingramcontent.com/pod-product-compliance
Lightning Source LLC
Chambersburg PA
CBHW051847170626
46807CB00003B/1389